IT'S BEGINNING TO HURT

IT'S BEGINNING TO HURT

James Lasdun

Farrar, Straus and Giroux

New York

Farrar, Straus and Giroux
18 West 18th Street, New York 10011

Copyright © 2009 by James Lasdun
All rights reserved
Distributed in Canada by Douglas & McIntyre Ltd.
Printed in the United States of America
Originally published in 2009 by Jonathan Cape Ltd., Great Britain
Published in the United States by Farrar, Straus and Giroux
First American edition, 2009

These stories first appeared, in various forms, in the following publications: *A Public Space* ("The Old Man"), *Granta* ("Caterpillars"), *New Writing* ("Peter Kahn's Third Wife"), *Open City* ("The Natural Order"), *Ploughshares* ("Cleanness"), *Prospect* ("The Woman at the Window," "A Bourgeois Story"), *Southword* ("The Half Sister"), *The Paris Review* ("An Anxious Man," "Oh, Death"), *Times Literary Supplement* ("Cranley Meadows," "Annals of the Honorary Secretary"), and *The Yale Review* ("Lime Pickle"). The story "It's Beginning to Hurt" was commissioned by Diana Reich for the Small Wonder Short Story Festival.

Library of Congress Cataloging-in-Publication Data
Lasdun, James.
    It's beginning to hurt / James Lasdun.— 1st American ed.
      p.   cm.
    ISBN-13: 978-0-374-29902-6 (alk. paper)
    ISBN-10: 0-374-29902-1 (alk. paper)
    1. Short stories.   I. Title.

PR6062.A735187 2009
823'.914—dc22

                                  2008054251

Designed by Jonathan D. Lippincott

www.fsgbooks.com

1   3   5   7   9   10   8   6   4   2

For Pia

Contents

IT'S BEGINNING TO HURT

An Anxious Man

Joseph Nagel slumped forward, head in hands.

"My God," he groaned.

Elise snapped off the car radio.

"Calm down, Joseph."

"That's four straight days since we got here."

"Joseph, please."

"What do you think we're down now? Sixty? Eighty thousand?"

"It'll come back."

"We should have sold everything after the first twenty. That would have been an acceptable loss. Given that we were too stupid to sell when we were actually ahead—"

Joseph felt the petulant note in his voice, told himself to shut up, and plunged on. "I did say we should get out, didn't I? Frankly it was irresponsible committing all that money"—shut up, shut up—"not to mention the unseemliness of buying in when you did—" oh God . . .

His wife spoke icily. "I didn't hear you complain when we were ahead."

"All right, but that's not the point. The point is . . ."

"What?"

Her face had tightened angrily on itself, all line and bone.

"The point is . . ." But he had lost his train of thought and sat blinking, walled in a thick grief that seemed for a moment unaccounted for by money or anything else he could put his finger on.

Elise got out of the car.

"Let's go for a swim, shall we, Darcy?"

She opened the rear door for their daughter and led her away.

Glumly, Joseph watched them walk hand in hand down through the scrub oaks and pines to the sandy edge of the kettle pond.

He gathered the two bags from their shopping expedition into his lap but remained in the car, heavily immobile.

Money . . . For the first time in their lives they had some capital. It had come from the sale of an apartment Elise had inherited, and it had aroused volatile forces in their household. Though not a vast amount—under a quarter of a million dollars after estate taxes—it was large enough, if considered a stake rather than a nest egg, to form the basis for a dream of real riches, and Joseph had found himself unexpectedly susceptible to this dream. The money he made as a dealer in antique prints and furniture was enough, combined with Elise's income from occasional Web design jobs, to keep them in modest comfort—two cars, an old brick house in Aurelia with lilac bushes and a grape arbor, the yearly trip up here to the Cape—but there wasn't much left over for Darcy's college fund, let alone their own retirement. In the past such matters hadn't troubled him greatly, but with the advent of Elise's inheritance he had felt suddenly awoken into new and urgent responsibilities. At their age they shouldn't be worrying about how to pay for medical coverage every year, should they? Or debating whether they could afford the dental and eye care package too? And wasn't it about time they built a studio so that Elise could concentrate on her painting?

The more he considered these things, the more necessary, as opposed to merely desirable, they had seemed, until he began to think that to go on much longer without them would be to accept failure, a marginal existence that would doubtless grow more pinched as time went by and end in squalor.

After probate had cleared and Elise had sold the apartment, they had gone to a man on Wall Street, a money manager who didn't as a rule handle accounts of less than a million dollars but who, as a special favor to the mutual acquaintance who had recommended him, had agreed to consider allowing the Nagels to invest their capital in one of his funds.

Morton Dowell, the man's name was. Gazing out at the pond glittering through the pines, Joseph recalled him vividly: a tanned, smiling, sapphire-eyed man in a striped shirt with white collar and cuffs and a pair of elasticized silver sleeve links circling his arms.

A young assistant, balding and grave, had shown them into Dowell's cherry-paneled bower overlooking Governors Island. There, sunk in dimpled leather armchairs, Joseph and Elise had listened to Dowell muse in an English-accented drawl on his "extraordinary run of good luck" these past twenty years, inclining his head in modest disavowal when the assistant murmured that he could think of a better word for it than "luck," while casually evoking image after image of the transformations he had wrought upon his clients' lives and hinting casually at the special intimacies within the higher circles of finance that had enabled him to accomplish these transformations.

"I think it's just so much fun to help people attain the things they want from life," he had said, "be it a yacht or a house on St. Bart's or a Steinway for their musical child . . ."

Joseph had listened, mesmerized, hardly daring to hope that this mighty personage would consent to sprinkle his magic upon their modest capital. He was almost overcome with gratitude when at the end of the meeting Dowell appeared to have decided they would make acceptable clients, sending his assistant to fetch his Sovereign Mutual Fund prospectus for them to take home.

"What a creep," Elise had murmured as they waited for the elevator outside. "I wouldn't leave him in a room with Darcy's piggy bank."

Stunned, Joseph had opened his mouth to defend the man but at once found himself hesitating. Perhaps she was right . . . He knew himself to be a poor judge of people. He, who could detect the most skillfully faked Mission desk or Federal-era sleigh bed merely by standing in its presence for a moment, was less sure of himself when it came to human beings. He tended to like them on principle, but his sense of what they were, essentially, was vague, unstable, qualities he suspected might be linked to some corresponding instability in himself. Whereas Elise, who had little interest in material things (and who had been altogether less unsettled by her inheritance than he had), took a keen, if somewhat detached, interest in other people and was shrewd at assessing them.

Even as their elevator began descending from Dowell's office, Joseph had found his sense of the man beginning to falter. And by the time they got home it had reversed itself entirely. Of course, he had thought, picturing the man's tanned smile and sparkling armbands again, what an obvious phony! A reptile! He shuddered to think how easily he had been taken in.

"You know what? You should invest the money yourself," he had told Elise.

"That had crossed my mind."

"You should do it, Elise! It can't be that hard." He was brimming with sudden enthusiasm for the idea.

"Perhaps I will give it a try."

"You should! You have good instincts. That's all that matters.

These money managers are just guessing like anyone else. You'd be as good as any of them."

And this in fact had appeared to be the case. After biding her time for several weeks, Elise had made her move with an audacity that stunned him. It was right after the September 11 attacks, when the shell-shocked markets reopened. Over ten days, as the Dow reeled and staggered, she bought and bought and bought, icily resolute while Joseph flailed around her, wrenched between his fearful certainty that the entire capitalist system was about to collapse, his guilty terror of being punished by the gods for attempting to profit from disaster, and his rising excitement, as the tide turned and he could see, on the Schwab Web page over his wife's shoulder, the figure in the Total Gain column swelling day after day in exuberant vindication of her instincts. An immense contentment had filled him. Thank God she had kept the money out of that fiend Dowell's clutches!

But then the tide had turned again. The number that had been growing so rapidly in the Total Gain column, putting out a third, a fourth, then a fifth figure, like a ship unfurling sails in the great wind of prosperity that had seemed set to blow once again across America, had slowed to a halt, lowered its sails one by one, and then, terrifyingly, had begun to sink. And suddenly Elise's shrewdness, the innate financial acumen he had attributed to her, had begun to look like nothing more than beginner's luck, while in place of his contentment, a mass of anxieties began teeming inside him . . .

How exhausting it all was. How he hated it! It was as though, in investing the money, Elise had unwittingly attached him by invisible filaments to some vast, seething collective psyche that never rested. Having paid no attention to financial matters before, he now appeared to be enslaved by them. When the Dow or NASDAQ went down, he was dragged down with them, unable to enjoy a beautiful day, a good meal, or even his nightly game of checkers with his daughter. Almost worse, on the rare occasions when the indices went up, a weird stupor of happiness would seize him, no matter what awful things might be going on around him. And more than just his mood, the management of his entire sense of reality seemed to have been handed over to the markets. Glimpsing in the *Times* business section (pages that would formerly have gone straight into the recycling bin) an article on mutual funds bucking the downward trend, he had seen Morton Dowell's Sovereign Fund among the lucky few and felt suddenly like a fool for having allowed what at once seemed an act of astoundingly poor judgment to steer him away from that sterling, agile man . . .

God! All that and the nightmarish discovery that you could never get out once you were in anyway, couldn't sell when you were ahead because you might miss out on getting even farther ahead, couldn't sell when you were down because the market might come surging back the next week, leaving you high and dry with your losses, though of course when it merely continued tanking, you wanted to tear your hair out for not having had the humility to acknowledge your mistake and salvage, sadder but wiser, what you could . . .

Whatever you did, it seemed you were bound to regret doing it, or not having done it sooner . . . It was as though some malicious higher power, having inspected the workings of the human mind, had calibrated a torment for it based on precisely the instincts of desire and caution that were supposed to enable it to survive. One could no more help oneself than the chickadee that nested in the lilacs outside their living room could stop attacking its own reflection in the window all day long every spring, however baffling and terrible every headlong slam against the glass must have felt.

Wearily, Joseph climbed out of the car.

In the kitchen, as he unpacked the grocery bags, he made a conscious effort to fight off his gloom. Four days into the vacation, and he had yet to relax. It was absurd. The weather was perfect, the rented house peaceful, the freshwater pond it stood by clear as glass, the ocean beaches beyond it magnificent. And at three hundred dollars a day for the house alone he couldn't afford not to be enjoying himself . . .

His hand made contact with a soft, cold package inside one of the bags. Ah yes. Here was something one could contemplate with unequivocal relish: a pound and a half of fresh queen scallops for the grill tonight.

He had bought them at Taylor's, while Elise and Darcy shopped at the produce store next door.

Taylor's was one of the glories of the Cape, and as always, it had been packed that afternoon, vacationers crushed up against the zinc slope, anxiously eyeing the diminishing piles of snowy-white bass fillets or glistening pink tuna steaks, guarding their place in line with one foot while peering ahead to see what sandy gold treasures lay in the day's salver of smoked seafood.

There had been an incident: two women had each laid claim to the last pair of lobsters in the tank. The woman who was first in line had been distracted, searching for something in her purse, when the teenage server came over. The other woman, tall and bronzed, in an outfit of some tissuey material slung weblike between thin chains of beaded gold, had silently held up two fingers and pointed to the lobsters, which the boy was already weighing for her when the first woman realized what was happening. She protested that she had been first in line, but the other woman simply ignored her, handing the boy several bills with an intense smile and telling him to keep the change, while the boy himself stood in a kind of paralysis that seemed as much to do with her immaculately constructed glamour training itself upon him at full beam as with the awkwardness of the situation. "We'll be gettin' more in later," he had muttered lamely to the first woman. "Well, gosh . . ." she had said breathily as the other woman, still smiling, strode serenely out, the two live lobsters swinging from her hand in their bag of crushed ice.

Joseph, who had observed it all, had felt vaguely that he ought to stand up for the woman in front. But nobody else had stirred, and it didn't after all seem a matter of great importance, so that in the end he had done nothing, a fact of which he had felt fractionally ashamed as he left the store.

At any rate he had his scallops—huge, succulent ones, with their delicate-tasting pink corals still attached. Lucky he'd bought them before hearing the day's numbers, he thought, smiling a little. Otherwise he might have balked at the astronomical price Taylor's charged per pound. He stowed them away with a feeling of minor triumph, as if he had snatched them from the very jaws of the NASDAQ.

———

There was no sign of his wife and daughter when he made his way down to the pond. He stood on the small private jetty that came with the house, wondering if he were being punished for his comment about the timing of Elise's investments. Elise did have a punitive streak, and his comment had undoubtedly been offensive. Still, it was unlike her to vanish altogether without telling him.

A slight anxiety stirred in him. He fought it: he had noticed a growing tendency to worry recently, and he was aware that he needed to get a grip on it. They must have gone off to pick blackberries, he told himself, or maybe they had decided to walk over the dunes to the ocean. At any rate he would have his swim—across the pond and back—before he allowed himself to become concerned.

He stepped into the clear water, walked out up to his knees, then plunged on in, drawing himself forward with leisurely strokes.

The top few inches of water were sun warmed; below that it was abruptly cold. There were no other people around. Thumbnail-size water skimmers teemed on the surface ahead of him: thousands of them, jetting twitchily in every direction.

The "pond" (he would have called it a lake) was a quarter mile wide. It took him twenty minutes to cross it, and by a determined effort of will he managed not to look back once to see whether Elise and Darcy had returned. At the far shore he climbed out to touch land, then turned around, half believing that he would be rewarded for his self-control by the sight of figures on the jetty below their house.

There were none.

Easy now, he instructed himself as he waded in again. There was still the journey back before he was officially allowed to worry. But knowing that in twenty minutes you were going to legitimately succumb to anxiety was not very different from succumbing to it right now. He could feel in advance how as he passed the halfway point on the pond, he would be seized by a mounting anger at Elise for not informing him of her plans and how as he swam on, the anger would change gradually to fear, which was worse because it indicated—did it not?—that one's mind had reached some limit of reasonable hope and switched its bet from her and Darcy's being perfectly, if irresponsibly, safe somewhere to their being caught up in some disaster . . .

How wearying, how humiliating it was to have so little faith in anything, to be so abjectly at the mercy of every tremor of fear in one's mind . . . Unballasted by any definite convictions of his own (convictions, he liked to joke, were for convicts), he appeared to have gone adrift in a realm of pure superstition. If I avoid listening to *Marketplace* for three days, the Dow will miraculously recover: it did not. If I close my eyes and hold my breath for seventeen strokes, Elise and Darcy will be there on the jetty . . .

They were not.

He swam on, thrusting out violently from his shoulders, ropes of cooler water slipping around his ankles as he kicked back and down, as hard as he could, in an effort to annihilate the drone of his own thoughts.

The sun was low in the sky, banding every ripple he made with a creamy glaze. The light here! That was something else to relish. In the early morning it seemed to glow from inside the trees, spilling out from one leaf after another as the sun rose: a rich, gold-tinted green. In the afternoon it turned to this creamy silver. Then it was the light itself one became aware of, rather than the things it lit. Right now, in fact, as Joseph looked across the pond, the glare of direct and water-reflected light was so bright he could no longer see the far shore. This seemed propitious, and he deliberately refrained from trying to squint through the dazzle, surrendering to it. He had caught this moment once or twice before on the pond, and it did have some mysterious, elevating splendor about it that took you out of yourself. Everything seemed purely an occurrence of light: the water streaming glassily as he raised each arm for its stroke, bubbles sliding over the curving ripples; the water skimmers registering no longer as frantic insect hordes but as careening saucers of light; the whole glittering mass of phenomena so absorbing it emptied your senses of anything but itself, and for a moment you had the impression you could not only see the light but taste it, smell it, feel it on your skin, and hear it ringing all around you like shaken bells.

Darcy was standing at the end of the jetty when he came through the glare. She was leaning over the water with a fishing net in her hand. Another girl was beside her, shorter and plumper, holding a yellow bucket. Behind them, a little farther off along the beach, sat Elise, drawing in her sketchpad.

For a moment Joseph tried to resist the joyful relief that the sight offered (relief being just the obverse of the irrational anxiety of which he was trying to cure himself and therefore equally undesirable), but it flooded into him. They were there! No harm had come to them! He swam on happily. How lithe and supple his daughter looked in her swimsuit, her legs growing long now, beautifully smooth, her brown hair already streaked gold from the sun.

A surge of love came into him, and with it a feeling of shame. How crazily out of perspective he had let things get, to have allowed money to loom larger in his mind than his own daughter! A few evenings ago she had been telling him in detail the plot of a film she had seen. He had pretended to be paying attention, but so preoccupied had he been with the day's losses that even his pretense had been a failure. With a pang he remembered the look of dismay on Darcy's face as she realized he wasn't listening to a word she was saying. How could he have done that? It was unforgivable!

The girls darted off as he approached the jetty, running down a path that led around the pond. Elise remained on her deck chair. She greeted him with a friendly look.

"Did you make it all the way across?" she asked.

"All the way. I see Darcy found a friend."

"Yes. She's staying in the next house down. We're invited over for cocktails later on."

"Cocktails. My!"

"I said we'd go. Darcy's so excited to have a playmate."

"Is she bored here?"

"No, but you know how it is . . ."

"I thought we might rent bikes tomorrow and go whale watching."

"Interesting concept."

"What? Oh!"

She was smiling at him. He laughed. Another of life's unequivocal pleasures: being reinstated in his wife's good graces. He rubbed himself dry. He felt refreshed, light on his feet.

———

An hour later he and Elise walked over to join their daughter at her new friend's house. A tall woman carrying a pitcher of purplish liquid greeted them on the deck.

"They call this a Cape Codder," she said, holding her free hand out to Joseph. "Hi, I'm Veronica."

She was the woman he had seen earlier on in Taylor's.

She had changed out of the tissuey top into a sleeveless robe of flowing peach-colored linen, but Joseph had recognized her at once as the victor in the incident with the lobsters.

She poured the drinks and called into the house: "Sugar . . ."

An older man came out onto the deck, sunburned, with a strong, haggard face and vigorous silvery tufts sprouting at his open shirt. "Hal Kaplan," he said, gripping Joseph's hand and baring a row of shiny white teeth in a broad smile.

Veronica poured drinks, and the four adults sat at a steel table on the deck, while the girls played down by the pond. She spoke rapidly, her large eyes moving with an intent sociability between Elise and Joseph. Within minutes she had sped the conversation past the conventional pleasantries to more intimate questions and disclosures, in which she took an unashamedly flagrant delight. She and Hal were each other's third spouse, she volunteered; they had met on a helicopter ride into the Grand Canyon. The girl, Karen, was Hal's daughter by his second wife, who had died in a speedboat crash. He and Veronica had been trying for a year to have a child of their own. There wasn't anything physically wrong with either of them, but because she was approaching forty and they didn't want to risk missing out, they had decided to sign up at an expensive clinic for in vitro fertilization, a process she described in droll detail, down to her husband's twenty-minute sojourns in the "masturbatorium." Don't mind me, her tone seemed to signal as she probed and confided. I'm not someone you have to take seriously . . . "How about you guys?" she asked. "How did you meet?" As he answered, Joseph found himself thinking that if he hadn't seen her in Taylor's earlier on, he would have taken her for precisely the charmingly frivolous and sweet-natured person she seemed intent on appearing. And in fact he so disliked holding a negative view of people that he rapidly allowed his present impression of her to eclipse the earlier one.

Hal, her husband, had been an eye surgeon in Miami for twenty-five years. Now he was living, as he put it, on his wits. To judge from the house they'd rented—bigger, sleeker, and glassier than Elise and Joseph's—he was doing all right on them.

"Karen is in love with your daughter," Veronica said to Elise, "she is in love with her."

Elise murmured that Darcy was thrilled too.

Swallows were diving over the pond, picking off skimmers. As the sun went down behind the trees, the water turned a greenish black, with a scattering of fiery ripples. The girls came up, wrapped in towels, shivering a little. Elise looked at her watch.

"Why don't you stay and eat dinner with us?" Veronica asked.

Elise smiled. "Oh no, we couldn't possibly . . ."

"It'd be no trouble, really."

"Say yes, Mommy!" Darcy cried.

"We're just throwing some things on the grill. It seems a shame to break these two up . . ."

"Daddy could bring over our scallops . . ."

Elise turned to Joseph. Assuming her hesitancy to be nothing more than politeness, he made what he thought was the expected gesture of tentative acceptance.

"Well . . ."

And a few minutes later he was bringing the scallops over from their kitchen, along with a bottle of wine.

Hal had lit the grill. Joseph poured himself another Cape Codder and joined him.

"Lousy day on the markets," he said, with a rueful chuckle.

The older man's long, rectangular face, full of leathery corrugations, hoisted itself into a grin.

"You play them?"

"We have a few little investments here and there."

"Time to buy more, is what I say."

"Oh? You think it'll go back up?"

"Like a rocket."

"Really? Even the NASDAQ?"

"No question. The smart money's all over it. I'm buying like crazy right now."

"You are?" Joseph's heart had given a little leap.

"You bet! Intel at twenty? Lucent under four dollars? These are bargain basement prices by any estimation. Nortel at two fifty? Not buy Nortel at two dollars and fifty cents a share?" He gave another grin, the centers of his lips staying together while the edges flew apart, showing his teeth.

"That's extremely interesting," Joseph said, enjoying the unexpected feeling of well-being that had come into him. "So you think a recovery's imminent?"

"Right around the corner, my friend. Right around the corner."

It was like drinking a draft of some fiery, potent liquor!

Hal jostled at the coals in the barbecue with a two-pronged fork. He called over to Veronica: "Bring 'em on, sweetheart!"

Veronica went into the kitchen and came out with the bag from Taylor's. Setting it on the table, she reached into the crushed ice and pulled out the two lobsters, one in each hand, and brought them over to the grill.

"Joseph, do me a favor and take the bands off, would you?" She was holding the creatures out toward him.

Gingerly, he removed the yellow elastic bands from the flailing blue claws.

"Careful," the woman said.

She caught his eye, giving him a sly, unexpected smile. Then she placed the living lobsters on the grill. Joseph had never seen this done before. The sight of them convulsing and hissing over the red hot coals sent a reflexive shudder of horror through him, though a few minutes later he was happily eating his share.

———

At three that morning he woke up with a dry mouth and a full bladder. He got out of bed and walked unsteadily toward the bathroom. Through the open door to the living room he glimpsed the sofa bed where Darcy slept and was momentarily stalled by the realization that it was empty. Then he remembered that she was sleeping over at her new friend's house.

A murky sensation, compounded of guilt and dim apprehension, stirred in him at the recollection of how this had come about.

He stumbled on into the bathroom, relieved himself, then stood in darkness, looking out at the pond. The moon had risen, and the surface of the water, dimpled here and there by rising fish, shone brightly in its ring of black trees.

He had drunk too much, that was for sure, and overeaten.

He recalled the weirdly euphoric mood that had mounted in him over the course of the evening, an unaccustomed exuberance. Partly it was Hal's amazingly confident predictions for the market. Several times Joseph had found himself steering the conversation back to the subject, raising various objections to the optimistic view, but purely for the joy of hearing this weather-beaten old oracle shrug them off. And partly too it was Veronica. With a few glances and touches she had deftly set a little subterranean current flowing between the two of them over dinner. He was a faithful husband, not even seriously tempted by actual bodily infidelity, but it gave him a tremendous lift to be flirted with by an attractive woman. Actually she wasn't, inherently, as attractive as he had first thought. Her chin was long, and her nose looked as though it had been broken. But her evident conviction that she was desirable appeared to be more than enough to make her so. By the end of the evening he had been in an exhilarated state, drunk, aroused, glutted, his vanity flattered, his head spinning with the thought of the markets shooting back up "like a rocket."

As they had stood up to leave, Elise had called Darcy, only to be informed by the girls that Karen had invited her for a sleepover and that she had accepted.

"Not tonight," Elise had said, with more firmness than Joseph had thought altogether polite to their hosts.

The girls began appealing at once to the other adults. Veronica took up their case, assuring Elise that Darcy would be more than welcome.

"We love having kids stay over. Anyway, we're only a hundred yards away . . ."

Elise had looked to Joseph for support. Simultaneously Veronica had turned to him. "It'll be so much fun for them, don't you think . . . ?" She had laid her hand on his arm, and in the flush of his dilated spirits, he had announced imperiously that since they were on vacation, he saw no reason why Darcy should not sleep over.

Elise had said nothing; it wasn't her style to argue in public. But as soon as they were out of earshot, leaving their daughter behind with her new friend, she had turned on Joseph with a cold fury. "First you force us to have dinner with those people, then you walk right over me with this sleepover. You are unbelievable."

More than the fierceness of her tone, more than the aggrieved wish to remind her that it was she, not himself, who had accepted the original invitation to go over for cocktails, more than the bewilderment at her objecting so strongly to Darcy's sleeping over with her new friend, it was her phrase "those people" that had startled him. All this time, he realized, while he had been blithely enjoying himself, she had been assessing this couple, sitting in judgment on them, and quietly forming a verdict against them. On what grounds? He had wanted to know. But as he opened his mouth to demand an explanation, he had felt once again the familiar sense of uncertainty about his own instincts.

And now, as he listened to the insomniac bullfrogs croaking down at the pond, the image of Veronica walking calmly out of Taylor's with the lobsters came back to him, and with a guilty wonder at his wife's powers of intuition, he went uneasily back to bed.

———

The day was overcast when he awoke later. He was alone. As he opened the curtains, he saw Elise striding up the steps from the pond. She burst in through the kitchen door.

"I am beyond angry."

"What happened?"

"They've gone."

"What do you mean?"

"They've gone. The car's not there."

"With Darcy?"

"Yes, with Darcy."

"No."

"Yes."

He felt a loosening sensation inside him.

"You checked inside the house?"

"The doors are locked. I yelled. There's no one there."

Joseph threw on his bathrobe and ran outside, racing down the steps to the path. Rain had begun pattering onto the bushes. Reaching the other house, he blundered about the deck, beating on doors and windows and calling Darcy's name. The place was empty. The windows had screens on the inside, making it hard to see into the unlit interior, but what he couldn't see with his eyes his imagination supplied vividly: empty rooms, everything packed swiftly and surreptitiously in the dead of night, Darcy bundled into the car with the rest of them, then off out into the vastness of the country.

A feeling of terror swelled up inside him. He staggered back along the path and up the steps, legs shaking, heart pounding in his chest. Elise was on the phone.

"Are you calling the police?"

She frowned, shaking her head.

If she wasn't calling the police, that must mean she didn't think things were as serious as he did. This calmed Joseph, though the calm had an artificial sheen to it that was familiar to him from the rare positive days on the Dow, as though some essential fact had been temporarily left out of the reckoning. Then he remembered again that Elise hadn't witnessed the scene in Taylor's, and it seemed to him suddenly that his wife had no idea what kind of people they were dealing with.

She hung up the phone and dialed another number. He realized she was calling nearby restaurants to see if their daughter's abductors had perhaps just gone out for breakfast. The idea seemed unbearably naive to him. He stood there, helpless, immobilized, looking out through the thickening rain.

She hung up again. "So much for that."

"What are we going to do?"

"What do you propose, Joseph?"

"I think we should call the police. What kind of car did they have?"

"For God's sake! I don't even remember their surname."

"Call the police."

"And say what? You call them."

He picked up the receiver but found himself reluctant to dial, as though to do so would be to confer more reality on the situation than he was ready to bear.

"Maybe just one of them went out and the other's still around here somewhere with the girls."

"Doing what?"

"I don't know. Picking blackberries . . . or maybe they went to the ocean . . ."

"In this?"

"It wasn't raining earlier. Why don't I go check? You wait here . . ."

He ran out of the house again. The sandy path wound around the pond to a series of dunes, the trees giving way to wild roses, then to sea grass with sharp edges that cut against his ankles. The sand crumbled under his feet as he climbed, half a step down for every step up. He was panting heavily as he reached the high point. Wind whipped rain and salt spray into his face. He looked down at the shore. On sunny mornings the narrow margin between the dunes and the waves would already be covered with towels and fluttering beach umbrellas and little human figures in bright swimsuits—a touching image, it always seemed to Joseph: life blossoming fraily between two inhospitable elements. It was empty now, not a figure visible on the mile-long stretch of wet sand. Black waves came racing in with the wind, exploding onto the shore. Gulls flew screeching over the surf.

Was this it? Was this the catastrophe he had felt preparing itself inside him? His obscure, abiding sense of himself as a flawed
and fallen human being seemed suddenly clarified: he was guilty,
and he was being punished. A feeling of dread gripped him.
Childlike thoughts arose in his mind: propitiation, sacrifice . . .
There was a clock, a valuable Crystal Regulator clock, that he had
bought for a bargain in Asheville earlier that year. If their daughter was at the house by the time he got back, he would sacrifice the
clock. He would destroy it, smash it to pieces in the back room of
his store. Or no, better, he would return it to the dealer who had
sold it to him, ask his forgiveness for taking advantage of him . . .
And meanwhile, to show he wasn't only prepared to make a sacrifice in return for a guaranteed reward (the primitive religious
state he had fallen into appeared to come complete with its own
finer points of dogma), he vowed, right there and then, to change
his entire life. Yes, he would devote himself to the poor and needy,
give up drinking, overeating, flirting, obsessing about the markets;
in fact he would tell Elise to sell off the shares, and they would
swallow the losses . . . The thought of this filled him with a sharp,
almost painful elation; he seemed to glimpse in it the possibility
of a new existence, one of immense and joyous calm. And even
though he was aware in another part of himself that there was no
prospect of his keeping a single one of these vows (that clock was
earmarked to pay for this vacation), he turned back along the path
full of faith and hope.

Veronica was at the house with the two girls when he arrived
back. She was talking to Elise on the deck outside the kitchen. Seeing Joseph, she waved, laughing.

"We were playing in a treehouse in the woods," she called out.
"Hal drove into town to buy pastries."

"Ah!"

"We always lock the door. Hal likes to keep a lot of cash around."

"I see. I see."

"We headed back as soon as we heard you guys yelling . . ."

She grinned at Joseph as he stepped onto the deck. She was wearing a white T-shirt and gold sneakers, her bare legs golden against the gray rain. A mischievous look appeared on her face:

"What were you thinking?"

He had had a moment of relief on seeing his daughter, but now he felt embarrassed.

"Nothing . . . We were just, you know, wondering where you were."

She touched his arm. "We freaked you out, huh?"

"No, no . . ."

He turned away, as though from an uncomfortably bright glare. Mumbling an excuse, he went on into the kitchen. Already his panic on the beach seemed absurd, shameful almost. What a state to get into! He turned on the radio. *Marketplace Morning Report* was about to come on. He lifted a watermelon from the fridge, set it on the counter, and cut himself a thick slice. He ate it nervously while he listened.

THE NATURAL ORDER

"So, do you always wear your wedding ring?"

"I do."

"I would never wear one of those things. The way it announces you're someone else's property."

"Shall we go on here or up to the gorge?"

"The gorge."

Abel took the turn that led off to the high part of the gorge. The landscape was thickly wooded, with the granite-walled gash of a nine-mile gorge cutting through the green slopes of the mountains.

"And you've never actually been unfaithful to Antonia in all the time you've been married?"

"No."

"Not even last night, eh?"

"What?"

"Just asking."

They came to the end of the tarmac road and began bumping over a narrow stone trail that climbed through a scrub of yellow-flowering broom. Strange rock formations—little citadels of thin, tall, wind-eroded towers—appeared on either side of the road. Stewart asked Abel to stop the car so that he could get out and photograph them.

Alone in the car, Abel watched Stewart jump lightly from rock to rock, camera in one hand, tripod in the other. A dull glare of hostility burned in him. He had known Stewart through mutual friends since the Scotsman's first arrival in the States several years earlier, but they'd never been close until these past three weeks on the road together, which had forced them into an intimacy that Abel had quickly found disturbing. Specifically, it was Stewart's ceaseless and exclusive preoccupation with sex that had unnerved him.

Not that it was entirely a surprise; in a vague way Abel had always known of Stewart's reputation as a ladies' man. And although he'd tended not to believe most of the stories he'd heard—girls accosting Stewart on the street, breaking into his apartment, picked up in cafés and bedded without a word spoken between them—he had certainly noticed that women were drawn to Stewart. He was tall and narrow-hipped, with the rare combination of black hair and blue eyes, the hair curling in thick clusters, the eyes mirthful, with a hint of laconic cruelty. His face, always clean-shaven, looked both angular and polished smooth, like some fine artifact constructed purely for the purpose of making a hand want to caress it. He wore brightly colored silk shirts that must have consumed an inordinate share of his income as a not very successful freelance photographer.

Early in the trip, Abel had realized that the stories were more likely to have been understatements than exaggerations. He had never been in a position to study the habits of a serious womanizer before, and what he'd observed had been a revelation.

The day after they'd arrived in Athens, a girl in a blue leather jacket had noticed Stewart in the hotel lobby (Abel had observed the brief, involuntary stilling of her glance as she crossed the floor).

The next morning Abel saw Stewart handing the leather jacket to the desk clerk.

"Wee thing split before I woke," Stewart had told Abel nonchalantly. "Left her jacket behind."

A few days later, in Meteora, they had both noticed a young Chinese woman leading a tour group up to one of the monasteries. By nightfall Stewart had found the woman again, discovered she spoke English, and invited her to join him and Abel for an after-dinner drink. Her manner was almost American in its casual ease, though Abel noticed that she held his eyes longer when she turned to him than most American women did. Not flirtatiousness, he sensed, so much as a remote, dispassionate interest, one empire taking the measure of another. Even so, he found himself trying to make her turn toward him as often as he could. He wasn't aware of competing with Stewart in this regard, but when the girl got up to leave, and Stewart offered to walk her back to her hotel, and she accepted without a word of protest as though this had long ago been settled between them, Abel had felt a distinct pang. He and Stewart were sharing a room that night, and in the small hours Abel was woken by the Scotsman's return. Stewart was laughing quietly, not drunk but lit up in some way.

"Smell that," he'd said, holding out his hand. "Chinese pussy."

A mass of sensations had erupted in Abel as the pungent aroma wafted from Stewart's fingertips: shock, vague anger, and hunger, envy too.

"She wouldn't let me go the whole way, though. Can you fucking believe it?" Stewart laughed again. Pacing the room in his vivid shirt and black jeans, he looked coiled and taut, with a wildness about him, an intent, sharp vitality that Abel realized he hadn't fully acknowledged until now.

One night they'd met two English girls, backpackers in their early twenties, up from a month of raves and beach parties on the islands. One had shaven blond bristles and a stud in her nose. The other was tall and dreamy-eyed, hennaed ringlets falling to her bare midriff. Within a few minutes Stewart had made his characteristic first move on the tall one, a jocular insult carefully calibrated to raise the temperature between them to the point where they became implicated in what, to all intents and purposes, was a lovers' quarrel, one that presupposed the tendernesses that invariably followed.

"I've never met an English girl who wasn't deep down just obsessed with getting married . . ."

"That's so unfair!"

The other girl glanced at Abel. He noticed a sweetness about her face that hadn't been immediately apparent under the bristles and stud. Her cheeks looked soft as a child's, her tawny eyes friendly. He thought of Antonia and the baby back in Connecticut. Where would they be now? Outside probably, lazing on the porch or feeding the chickens. He tried to picture them. The girl impinged on him, producing a little hip flask and taking a swig from it . . .

"Greek brandy," he heard. "Totally lethal."

There had been a moment a few months ago when he and Antonia had been in the old barn where her father's travel book business was housed. Winter sunshine was melting the icicles outside the window, and in the sweet gelid light that filled the high-beamed room, Abel had been filled with unexpected euphoria. Watching his wife laying out pages, their swaddled child sleeping in the cradle beside her, he had been visited by stronger feelings of love than he had ever imagined himself capable of feeling. It was as though the full reality of his marriage—its brimming sufficiency—had for the first time been made radiantly apparent to him. The moment had passed, but the revelation had survived in him untarnished, lit with the gleam of the melting icicles, and filling him with contentment whenever he thought of it.

"Want a hit?" The girl was offering him her flask.

"Oh. No thanks."

"You're the quiet American, aren't you?"

"Excuse me? Oh . . . Not really, just the tired American."

He stood up, catching what appeared to be a brief flash of annoyance in the girl's eye as he made his excuses and left.

Up in his room he thought of her. Was it really possible that she could have been interested in him? He looked in the mirror, felt the familar jolt at the disparity between his persistently youthful idea of his physical appearance and the image that confronted him. His hair lay thinly over his temples; his torso looked shapeless in the useful lightweight beige anorak he had brought along for the cooler evenings. An *hors de combat* jacket, Stewart had jokingly called it when he first saw Abel sporting it . . . He smiled wanly at himself. He looked middle-aged.

Next morning he discovered that both of the girls had spent the night with Stewart.

Breakfasting with the three of them—him uncomfortable, not wanting to seem either prurient by talking about the night's outcome or priggish by conspicuously not alluding to it; them calm, sated-looking, globed in their mutual contentedness—he had felt both obscurely mocked and, even more obscurely, ashamed.

That was a week ago. Since then there had been a woman in a zip-up dress who worked in the tourist bureau in Thessaloniki, a bespectacled assistant in a camera store, the faded-looking proprietress of a small hotel . . . Not my business what he does, Abel had told himself, but he had begun to feel strangely oppressed. He had never thought of his state of contented monogamy as something unusual or in need of justification, but the effect of Stewart's behavior had been to make him feel as though he had consciously adopted some bizarre, almost freakish approach to life. He won-

dered for the first time whether his faithfulness as a husband had
been a matter of deliberate choice or passive acquiescence. Had he
deliberately suppressed the appetites of a potential philanderer for
the sake of a greater happiness, or had his life taken the shape it
had because he didn't have those appetites in the first place? Or
was it just that his love for Antonia was so strong that faithfulness
was simply what came naturally?

It occurred to him that at the very least there were things
about the Stewart approach to life that he could adopt without
compromising himself. For one thing, he could sharpen up his appearance. Being married didn't mean you had to relinquish all
claim to being regarded as a physical animal, but somehow he had
managed just that. His clothes had become shabby, formless, utili-
tarian. The luster and contour he had once taken care to maintain
had given way, he realized, to an apparent desire to blur himself
into the background of any given situation. He felt a sudden revulsion for the contents of his suitcase: dust-colored rags of baggy cotton and corduroy; the horrible beige anorak with its webby lining,
its pleated elastic waistband, and plastic black toggles. Forget *hors
de combat*; the thing was more like a body bag! But he had worn it
almost every evening of their trip . . . Christ! What had happened
to him?

They were in Kastoria, up near the Albanian border, giving
themselves a rest day. It was an old center for the fur trade; furri-
ers still lined the hilly streets, their fronts hung with the glossy
pelts of beaver, mink, ocelot, chinchilla . . . Not exactly what Abel
had in mind, but the sight confirmed his sense of the dereliction
of his own exterior.

He got a haircut in a barbershop, letting the barber slick back
his sparse locks with fistfuls of greenish gel. He bought three
linen shirts in rich colors and a pair of charcoal pants made of a

silky material that arranged itself around his legs with the fluid, blandishing lines of drapery on a classical statue. A suede jacket caught his eye in another window. He'd last had a suede jacket in his twenties, when he had gone to live in Europe for a couple of years. Looking at this one, he felt a keen craving to possess it. He went in, tried it on. It was a good fit, expensive but not extortionate. He bought it, paying cash in his eagerness to possess it, the thick wad of bills soft as the suede itself. Shoes: you couldn't wear these clothes with the all-purpose sneakers he had on, their squished quiltings and bulgings giving them the appearance of giant, misshapen caterpillars. He bought a pair of square-toed black shoes with chrome buckles. Not much use in the mountains, but there were other considerations after all . . .

Stewart was out when he got back to the hotel. Abel showered in the shared bathroom between their rooms and dried himself at the mirrored sink. Stewart's wash things were arranged around the rim of the sink. At the start of the trip, Abel had been struck by the quantity of toiletries that Stewart traveled with, but beyond a reflex twinge of condescending amusement, he hadn't given the matter any further thought. Now, though, as he looked at the array of conditioner jars, moisturizer tubes, bottles of shampoo, little beribboned vials of essential oils and aftershave lotions, the deodorant stone, the gleaming clippers, trimmers, and scissors, the elegant traveling razor and badger hair shaving brush, he felt again the full reality of Stewart's quietly fanatical dedication to his appearance, and this time found himself filled with something more like envy than condescension.

The thought struck him that Stewart, whom he had always vaguely thought of as his inferior, was in some sense—some important sense he had never properly considered—a higher order of being than himself. He flinched from the idea, felt strangely undone by it, almost wanted to utter a groan . . . But it was true: under the man's crassness a fine, bright flame seemed to burn in him. One was almost physically aware of it: a steady incandescence of sexual interest in the world, the lively brightness of which was its own irrefutable argument.

Was there, Abel found himself wondering, any possibility of attaining that quality himself? Had there ever been? More painful to contemplate: Had he ever even truly wanted it? That question seemed to bring with it from the depths some ancient, obscurely held suspicion about himself: that perhaps what he truly wanted was not to be alive at all and that failing that, he had done all he could to make his life approximate as closely as possible the condition of not being alive. Was that the real meaning of that icon of his wife and child, fixed in the gelid wintry light of his in-laws' barn: the swaddled child silently sleeping; his wife immobile, statuesque . . . Not presence of joy, but absence of pain: Was that what the domestic contentment he thought he had found amounted to? And if so, where had this strange inclination to be stone come from? Some insidious psychic wound? Or some more culpable failure of spirit? Had he chosen to become this way? Was it possible to change?

He opened a corked glass vial and sniffed: bay rum. He sprinkled a few drops in his hair and rubbed it in. Back in his room he dressed carefully in his new clothes: crimson linen shirt, the charcoal pants, the chrome-buckled shoes. The evening air was already cool enough to justify the suede jacket. Standing in it, he felt almost as he had a decade earlier, living a bohemian fantasy in Europe, setting out onto the streets of Copenhagen or Madrid for his evening wanderings, joyfully adrift, with a light, clear feeling of infinite promise.

He went downstairs to the restaurant.

Stewart was already there, eating *mezes* with a group of Americans.

"New haircut," he observed as Abel joined them. He took in the jacket, fingering the sleeve approvingly. "Well, well. Aren't we the semi-handsome dude tonight! Here, meet—what're all you's names?"

The Americans introduced themselves. They were hikers, on a tour of the northern mountains. Most of them looked in their fifties and sixties, prosperous couples, their clothes and gear hanging on them with the faint unassimilable stiffness of things bought from outdoor catalogs. But among them was a woman in her thirties, apparently on her own. She wore jeans and an old blue jean jacket. She had a droll, solicitous air, smiling attentively at her companions' remarks, but at the same time, Abel sensed, a bit depressed by them. Her name was Rose.

Stewart had established himself next to her at the table. He was talking to the whole group, regaling them with his and Abel's adventures on the road, but it was obvious whom the performance was intended for. He was playing out a routine Abel had seen before, his eloquent barbarian routine, which consisted of dusting off his accent and assuming the persona of a laconically blunt Scot.

"Anyway, the shitehead's clearly under the impression we've no got the balls to stand up to a big Balkan laddie like him, so my friend here, who I can assure you is normally the most docile of gentlemen, picks up the desk phone and starts dialing the tourist police. Well, the cunt goes all huffy . . ."

Glancing past his neighbor at the younger woman, Abel was surprised to see that she was looking at him. She smiled. Her eyes, under thick gold lashes, were the same faded blue jean color as her jacket. She appeared to be paying no attention to Stewart's story.

"You're writing a book?" she asked quietly.

"Oh . . . If you can call it a book. A guidebook."

"That's a book."

"Well . . ."

"Not *War and Peace*, right?"

He nodded; startled to find a stranger even remotely on his wavelength.

"I used to work in book publishing." She went on. "I quit to go live in the desert with one of my authors."

She laughed, apparently at her own folly. They leaned back in their chairs, defecting from the circle of Stewart's listeners. Before long, barely conscious of arranging it, Abel found himself at a separate table with her, with their own food and their own red metal jug of retsina gleaming between them. They were deep in conversation.

". . . We were getting slower and slower. Some mornings I could barely make it into the hammock. I'd just stand there looking at it, like I'd turned into a cactus or something. A bird could've built a nest on my shoulder. You live in Connecticut, you said?"

"Yes. But so what happened?"

"Oh, I don't know . . . Apparently I'm somewhere in the north of Greece on a hiking trip with some very nice folks twice my age, but I'm not exactly sure how I got here or why I came."

"I know the feeling."

At one point Stewart appeared at their table, holding a drink. His own table had broken up. Abel and Rose smiled at him, continuing their conversation. He pinched a fold of Abel's new shirt. "Suits him, don't you think, the crimson?"

"Yes, it does," Rose said.

"Bit John Travolta—ish, though. But maybe you're planning to show us some of your disco moves, Abel, later on?"

"Maybe."

Glancing from Abel to Rose, Stewart yawned suddenly and drifted off.

The two were silent a moment. Rose looked at him, the sun-faded blue of her eyes distantly welcoming. He felt the light pressure of her fingers on his hand.

"Is that a wedding ring?"

"Yeah."

She looked at him again; something quizzical now, tentatively wary in her expression. He held her gaze, steadily. It was like wandering down some long, warm trail, somewhere with dry, sweet-smelling, blue-domed air. He had been here before, or somewhere like it, though not in a long time. The warm, amused expression returned to her eyes. She projected a sense of being utterly alone in the world. Between the black of her pupils and the blue of her irises were yellowish flares, like the flaring rays of an eclipsed sun in the midday sky. The more he looked at her, the more unusual and likable and attractive she seemed. More attractive, he noted, than the women who were drawn to him usually were.

They finished their retsina. The restaurant began closing up. It seemed to Abel that he could see with absolute clarity what lay ahead. When they were ready, they would walk out onto the vine-trellised path that led from the hotel to the ruined fort overlooking the town. Up at the top they would go on talking for a while; then they would lie in silence listening to the night. Their hands would touch, take hold of each other . . . Later they would find themselves back in one of their rooms making love. And the next day they would go their separate ways, each heavy with the rich freight of a new human being inside them.

He had always thought that if he were unfaithful to Antonia, it would be under conditions of frenzied intoxication. But what he felt now was something calmer, more like the acceptance of some impersonal decree. It was simply something that was going to happen, a reality that had established itself.

———

"So how come you didn't fuck her?"

"For Christ's sake, Stewart."

"I mean you fancied her, right?"

"She was attractive, yeah."

"She fancied you too."

"How do you know?"

"She told me."

It was two days later, and Abel was in a black mood. He looked at Stewart a moment in the mirror but said nothing.

They were on their way to Zagoria, the last leg of their trip. The hills with their knots of dusty-looking olive trees grew taller and greener, the air a little cooler. The rented car slowed to a crawl as the straight road began its switchback ascent into the gorge country of Epirus.

Already his actions of that evening had begun to seem obscure to Abel. He doubted even the accuracy of what still seemed relatively clear in recollection. One moment he had been in the full momentum of a trajectory about to sweep him and Rose out into the warm night; the next, he was lying alone on his bed with the sensation of having just committed some violently unnatural act. Had he said good night or just turned on his heel and disappeared? He had a bad feeling it might have been the latter, though the former seemed hardly less appalling to him. Out through the window of his room he had seen the scattered whiteness of the moon on the leaves of the vine trellis that led up from the hotel. Grapes hung in shadowy clusters. At that moment, had he not disappeared, he and Rose would have been walking slowly right there, perhaps reaching up to pluck one of the ripe bunches . . . He had almost felt that they were out there, that his being alone on his bed was a minor anomaly of nature, like the alleged ghostly presence of a particle in one place at the same time as it is being definitively observed in another. The version of himself out there with Rose had a far denser reality about it than this one did. But here he was . . . What he felt, more than the embarrassment at his own behavior, more even than the aborted desire ricocheting around inside him, was a feeling of loss. Life offered up so few human beings you could contemplate any intimacy with that to turn your back on one seemed an insane and profligate waste. He summoned the winter-lit image of his wife and child in the barn at home in Connecticut. For once nothing stirred in him. The image seemed flat, as though it had spent all its powers bringing him back from the brink of some abyss and was now just a lifeless reproduction of itself.

"When did she . . ." Abel heard himself begin to ask, though he had resolved not to. "When did she tell you?"

"Tell me what?"

"That she . . . found me attractive."

Stewart gave a lopsided smile.

"Oh, after you left her."

"I thought you'd gone to bed." Drop it, Abel admonished himself.

"I saw her down on the terrace, sitting there all by herself. She looked like she could use some company."

"So you went down?"

"Yeah, I went down."

Stewart eyed him in the mirror: a semblance of laconic friendliness, but under it something remote, self-possessed, almost haughtily indifferent. He offered no further comment, and Abel tried to refrain from further questions.

"Did you fuck her?" he blurted.

Stewart was silent a moment. Then quietly, almost gently: "What can I tell you? She wanted getting laid."

"I see."

"Does it bother you?"

"No! You can fuck whoever you want. Why would I care?"

"I get the feeling you do care."

"Well, you're wrong. I don't."

———

In the evening they arrived at a village above the gorge. Picturesque enough for their purposes but desolate. There had been atrocities there in the civil war: a massacre, then reprisals. The place was subsiding—willingly, it almost seemed—back into the mountain rubble it had risen from. Black-shawled old women stared from the doorways of the few houses that hadn't been boarded up. Scrawny poultry roosted on the stone path leading to the hotel where Abel and Stewart checked in, the only guests.

The next morning it was raining. Abel stayed in his room, working up the cheery platitudes required by his father-in-law's "Wild Europe" series: "From the slit-windowed fortress of a hotel, its stone tiles ragged-edged as the scales of a venerable old carp, you wind down steep cobbled alleys (watch out for guinea fowl!) to the lovely basilica of St. Nikos Dukas, a gem of Byzantine architecture . . ." As a younger man he'd had ideas of becoming a playwright, and although he'd long ago made his peace with the failure of that enterprise, shifting the basis of his happiness from the withheld trophies of the outer world to the freely given bounties of his domestic life, he took a perverse satisfaction in perpetrating these verbal banalities. Revenge by cliché . . .

But after a couple of hours he found himself yawning. He felt simultaneously restless and torpid. He wanted to be elsewhere, without knowing where. Home? It didn't seem so. The thought of home felt thin and theoretical. He would be back there in three days, and then, he supposed, it would all be real enough. But for now the whole notion of it—wife, child, in-laws, the peaceful routine of their days in the old farmstead—had gone dormant in him. He was bored too, without knowing what he wanted to do. Big airy columns of rain floated down against the mountains and on into the distant gray depths of the gorge. He found himself thinking of Rose. He saw again the look of warm, candid welcome in her blue eyes. A helpless yearning came into him. Apparently she really had been offering herself to him. He had wanted her and yet had refused her. The correct thing for a happily married man to do. But it seemed to him, now, that in observing the human protocol, he had violated some wider law of nature. Why else the obscure, dank sensation of shame clinging to him?

He saw that the encounter was going to take its place among the events that made up his fundamental sense of what he was. A depressing thought, given the distinct mediocrity of spirit it seemed to manifest . . . He got up. Maybe a walk in the rain would do him good.

There in the drawer lay his trusty anorak, self-effacingly pouched into one of its own pockets. He put it on, the beige nylon as forgiving and shapeless on him as a dust sheet on an old chair, something insidiously reassuring about its familiar embrace.

As he came down the stairs, he heard laughter, female, ringing loudly over the unadorned stony surfaces of the hotel. Stewart was at a table in the lobby, opposite two women.

An incredulous jolt, a kind of pang, went through Abel. He had heard no car pull up, no bustle of arrival . . . Where on earth had the man conjured these creatures from?

"Come and join us," Stewart called, waving him over.

"Well, I was just going for a walk."

"Ach, we'll go later. Melina here says it's going to clear up in an hour. Right, Melina?" He grinned superciliously at one of the women. "Melina's a psychic prophet. She's been reading the coffee grounds. She can also read your mind, so don't be having any dirty thoughts."

The high, full laughter rang out again. Abel saw glasses of ouzo on the table, along with cups of Greek coffee. He wasn't in the mood for a party. But short of maintaining an attitude of extreme churlishness, he was clearly going to have to join them sooner or later.

He went reluctantly over to the table. Stewart introduced them. Melina was fair-haired and large—not fat, but swollen-looking somehow, as though by a superfluous creaminess in her silvery-pale flesh. Her soft white arms were dimpled at the elbow, and there were dimples either side of her pale lips. Her eyes were a deep green color. Abel watched them travel over him briefly, taking in his sparse hair, his lined face, the toggled and zippered shroud of his beige anorak. She turned away. At one of her wrists was a frill of pink silk. Her plump hands and tapering, jointless-looking fingers had the smooth solidity of limbs cast in wax. Rings of opal and tiger's-eye glimmered on them, and with some fascination Abel noted a curious, two-fingered diamond-encrusted ring joining together the third and fourth fingers of her right hand.

The other woman, Xenia, was sallow and angular, with a bony, almost cartilaginous face, the olive skin taut over her little, sharp nose, her ears small but protuberant, like the ears of some nervous tree creature. They looked as if they might swivel. Her dark eyes settled a moment on Abel's.

Stewart ordered him some coffee.

"We'll have Melina read your fortune. She's been predicting all kinds of catastrophes for yours truly. Tell him what you told me, Melina."

Melina turned lazily to Abel. "He's going to be married before the year's over."

"Oh, really?"

"Yes. He's going to settle down in a big house with a view over a harbor, and he's going to be faithful to his wife for the rest of his life."

"Apparently I'm to marry the next woman I kiss," Stewart said with a chuckle.

The woman turned back to him: statuesque, at ease in her slightly bulky softness.

"Well, it's true. You are." She smiled complacently at him.

A one-armed old man brought coffee for Abel. Melina spoke to him in Greek, and he nodded.

"Drink that up," Stewart said, "and Melina'll tell us what the future holds for you."

"I don't think I want to know."

But he drank the grainy syrup and let Melina take the cup. She swirled the dregs so that the grounds clung to the inside of the white china. For a long moment she stared without expression into the cup.

"It's not good news," she said.

"Then I surely don't want to hear."

"Ah, come on," Stewart said. "It couldn't be worse than my little death sentence."

"He's going to be divorced. He's going to lose his home and his child. Also his job."

"Well, thanks," Abel said. "Lucky I'm not superstitious."

Melina looked at him. She seemed in a luxuriant stupor of indifference toward him.

"That's good," she said. "Then you don't have to believe it."

She ran her pampered-looking hands through her thick, soft wings of hair, one hand, then the other. A sweetish perfume wafted from her. The bunched silk on her wrist reminded Abel of the paper frills you used to see on the stumps of roasts in glossy food magazines.

The one-armed man returned to their table with a tray of pastries: baklava; little pistachio-eyed turbans; something that looked like a small manuscript dipped in custard. One thing Abel and Stewart were agreed on was their dislike of Greek pastries, and they both declined when Melina offered them around. She shrugged, unperturbed, and began eating them herself. Hampering her third and fourth fingers, the double ring looked less like jewelry than some curious splint. Xenia nibbled on one of the turbans.

The weather cleared abruptly. Stewart glanced at Abel. "We'll go check out the ridge then, shall we?"

As the men stood to go, the two women spoke to each other rapidly in Greek. Melina grinned at Stewart.

"We'd like to invite you to dinner tonight. Both of you." She spoke with the token coyness of someone evidently used to getting what she wanted. "We'll have the hotel prepare a little feast. Our treat, of course."

————

That had been yesterday. They had left the village this morning. Tomorrow they would be back in Athens, the next day home.

They came to a turning in the narrow road.

"Shall we go on here or up to the gorge?"

"The gorge."

Abel turned onto the smaller road.

"And you've never actually been unfaithful to Antonia in all the time you've been married?"

"No."

"Not even last night, eh?"

"What?"

"Just asking."

Here were the strange-looking wind-eroded rock towers.

"Mind stopping a moment? I should get some pictures."

Alone in the car, Abel watched Stewart jump between the rocks with his camera and tripod. He was in a state of tumult, glutted with sensations. It had been a warm evening, and they had dined outside. After keeping Abel and Stewart waiting an hour, the women showed up on the terrace in extravagant, gleaming outfits: a laced silver bodice on Melina, her midriff bare like a belly dancer's, loose linen pants flowing from her broad hips, silk frill at her wrist; Xenia in a mauve leather skirt and satin halter top, her freckled, bangled arms looking almost childlike in their thinness. They both wore high heels and makeup. Their hair had been freshly washed and set, and their mingled perfumes billowed ahead of them through the warm air, soft but full of forceful intent, like the scent that hits you as you enter the cosmetics section of a department store.

"What's this, singles night in the wilderness?" Stewart had asked.

Melina laughed and sat next to him, Xenia seating herself by Abel with a nervous smile that he interpreted to mean that she wasn't at ease in her getup.

"You look nice," he heard himself say, an uncharacteristic gallantry that sounded very strange to him as it came out, but for which she seemed grateful.

The women had laid on quite a feast. Champagne and island wines had been procured from the nearest town, fifteen miles away, and a young goat had been slaughtered.

They went rapidly through a couple of bottles of champagne, while the one-armed man brought out dishes of octopus and fried cheese.

"So we were wondering what you guys think we do, for a living," Melina said. "What do you think, Abel?"

Startled at finding himself for once being addressed by her, Abel blustered. "I—I have no idea . . ."

"You're a madam in a brothel," Stewart said, "and your friend here's a freelance assassin."

They shrieked with laughter. Jesus, Abel had thought, what kind of witless jackass have I turned into? He downed his glass while Melina continued: "Actually, we both work on Wall Street. We're investment consultants for a Greek bank. Would you like to guess how much we make in a year?"

"No," Stewart said, "but I think you'd like to tell us."

"A little over a million dollars."

"That's all?" Abel jumped in, seeing an opportunity to redeem himself. "I pay my driver more than that."

For this he earned an enthusiastic laugh from Xenia and a faint smile from Melina.

Xenia was smoking while she ate, and after his fifth or sixth glass of champagne, Abel decided to ask her for a cigarette, though he hadn't smoked in years. She gave him one, took another for herself, and handed him her lighter to light them both. As he held the flame to her cigarette, she cupped his hand, even though there was no breeze to speak of. He was aware of the ridiculously hackneyed nature of the little routine. At the same time—such, apparently, was the hackneyed nature of his response mechanism—he felt a jolt of desire go through him.

He looked into her strange face as he inhaled on his cigarette. She had a slight prematurely wizened look, as though she might have once been undernourished or anorexic. She wasn't in any sense his type, but he found himself drawn to her, narrowly, as though on a thin thread of mysteriously aroused erotic curiosity. The nicotine swam dizzyingly through his head. The sky had turned violet over the mountains. The one-armed man began hacking up the goat, which had been spit-roasting on a brazier.

"How d'you reckon he lost his arm?" Stewart said.

Melina at once asked the man. His weathered, wrinkled face whorled into a grin as he answered. He was fighting Communists, Melina translated; he was a sniper, used to pick them off in their fields from high in the mountains. Then they captured him, smashed his trigger finger. They were going to execute him, but he escaped. His hand got gangrene while he was hiding in the mountains. It spread all the way up his arm . . . The man burst into laughter and served up the goat.

"Killing Communists, eh?" Stewart said. "Serves him right then."

"The Communists were worse than the others," Melina retorted.

"What, are you a Nazi apologist as well as a capitalist pig?"

Stewart said this with a smile, and Melina responded with delighted outrage. They finished the goat, going through several more bottles in the process. Melina spoke to the one-armed waiter, who nodded and disappeared. A moment later there was a bray of harsh, rhythmic music—clarinet, accordion, drum—and a band of ragged-looking musicians appeared on the terrace.

"They're Albanians," Melina said under the din. "We found them in Ioannina."

"Jesus, it really is singles night," Stewart said.

"We thought you guys might like to dance."

"I don't dance with Nazis."

Melina opened her mouth to laugh but, seeing that Stewart wasn't smiling now, closed it and looked for the first time unsure of her ground.

"I will drink some more of your booze, though. Not that crappy vino. The Mumm's." He held his glass out to be filled. Instead of filling it, Melina passed him the bottle, frowning.

"Oho, a pouty Nazi!"

She said nothing. It wasn't clear to Abel if this was just Stewart's usual lovers' quarrel gambit. The idea of his not wanting to sleep with a woman because of her politics struck Abel as unlikely, but there was a glint of what seemed real malice in Stewart's eye. The four sat in silence. The musicians began stamping their feet and hooting, as if afraid of being dismissed if their patrons didn't liven up. More to break the tension than anything else, Abel invited Xenia to dance. She accepted with alacrity, and to the delight of the Albanians they took to the floor.

Abel had drunk enough not to feel any self-consciousness as he eased into the all-purpose, low-key shuffle he had perfected as a teenager and felt no subsequent need to embellish. Xenia danced before him, for him, it felt, twirling around, moving a few steps away, but only, it seemed, in order to be continually coming toward him. She held his eyes whenever she did, and the effect on him was powerful. He was aware of not finding her attractive and yet of feeling increasingly mesmerized by her. Out of the corner of his eye he noticed Melina in the candle glare of the table, watching them, while Stewart sat drinking in silence beside her. The musicians began playing a slow tune. Again Xenia moved toward him, this time with a tentative, questioning look in her eye. He took her hands and drew her close. The difference between just dancing with her and holding her was immense. His feeling of slight detachment from the situation vanished. With one hand on her small, naked, bony shoulder, the other hand lightly gripping hers, he felt for the first time in many years the vivid carnal reality of a woman other than his wife. The question of whether she was likable or even attractive no longer seemed relevant. He drew her closer, felt her hair brush silkily against his face, then the coolness of her skin against his cheek. His whole body seemed to dilate. Was saying yes instead of no to this all it took, he wondered drunkenly; all it consisted of, that superior vitality of Stewart's that he had seemed to glimpse back in Kastoria? Circling slowly around, he saw Stewart get up from the table.

"Bedtime for Stewart," Abel heard him mutter. "Thanks for the chow, girls. G'night . . ."

He swayed off into the hotel. Melina sat alone for a while, watching them, the frilled silk at her wrist rather tragic-looking now, like the bow on an unwanted present. She ran her hands through her hair, one hand, then the other. A little later Abel noticed that she too had disappeared.

———

The high mountain road oozed under their tires, softened by yesterday's rain. It ended abruptly at a narrow footpath. They got out and walked. The air smelled of wet, raw stone.

"What a pair, though. What a profoundly depressing pair. Hope we never get that desperate, eh?"

Abel said nothing.

"That Melina, Jesus! Someone should put a bell round her neck and milk her. As for the wee monkey—"

"—She seemed pretty hot for you. Melina, I mean."

"You noticed?" Stewart raised a sardonic eyebrow. "I had a midnight visitation from her. She comes into my room in this little pussy-high lace number, all fake teary-eyed, claiming she couldn't sleep because I'd upset her. I ended up having to let her give me a blow job."

"That must have cheered her up."

"I was fucked if I was going to fuck her. Christ, will you look at that!"

The path had come out at the gorge, an abrupt, sheer, granite-shaded plunge of nothingness. A lurch of vertigo went through Abel's stomach.

"All right?" he heard Stewart ask.

"Yeah."

"Afraid of heights?"

"No."

For a moment it was impossible to get a sense of the scale of what he was confronting. The thin glint way down under the furling mist: Was that a little stream or a full-size torrent?

"So the chimp . . . I really thought you were going to take one for the team there."

"Huh?"

"You know . . . Payback for the Mumm's. *Boff de politesse.*"

"If you mean you were thinking I slept with her, the answer is no, Stewart, I did not."

A formal denial, he thought as he heard himself uttering it. He wondered how convincing it had sounded. More to the point, how did it make him feel? Anxious? Guilty? He tried to picture himself back home with Antonia, telling the same lie or, if not telling it, living it . . . Was he really going to go back there and continue as if nothing had happened? A distant feeling of horror seized him, as in nightmares he sometimes had, where it was revealed to him that he had committed some unspeakable atrocity. There they were again in his mind's eye, fixed in the pale winter light of his in-laws' barn: the swaddled child silently sleeping; his wife all serene, marmoreal immobility, glazed somehow . . . Like the *Pietà* behind her glass screen, he thought, remembering a trip they'd made to Italy for her father's series, before the baby was born. They'd had to look at the sculpture through the bulletproof glass that had been put there after a man fired a gun in her face.

At the same time a feeling of elation was rising through him. All morning the sense of Xenia naked in his arms on the cool forest floor had been surging back through him in waves; her braceleted hands on his body, the hot musk scent of her throat and breasts as electrifyingly real in memory as they had been in the flesh. It was hard to tell whether he or she had been the more astonished by the sudden, almost frenzied desire for each other that had risen in them the moment he brought her willing mouth against his and kissed her, half deafened by the clamor of the Albanian band. Leaving the musicians to the one-armed waiter, they had stumbled off down through the trees till they fell on a bed of pine needles, unbuttoning and unzipping each other frantically, as if their apartness till now had been the result of a forced separation rather than the simple fact that they hadn't met. Penetrating her as she gripped the small of his back with her sharp-nailed, jangling hands, he had felt an unfamiliar savage jubilation. More like the pleasure of smashing something to pieces than of making love. Afterward they had gone to his room and slept together on the bed. When he awoke at dawn to leave for the gorge with Stewart, she was gone. But she had left her New York number on a scrap of paper by the bed, scribbled in what looked like crimson felt tip.

He had hardly spoken a word to her. He barely knew who she was, had no idea what he thought of her or whether he would want to see her again. In two days he would be home. He tried to imagine it, but his mind went blank. He put his hand in his pocket. There was the scrap of paper with the phone number. Get rid of it, he told himself; chuck it in the ravine . . . He looked over at Stewart,

who was busy setting up his camera, smiling to himself and whistl-
ing a little tune. Taking the paper from his pocket, Abel saw that
the number was in fact written in lipstick. The scent of Xenia's
mouth wafted from it, wavering through him like a hot, soft flame.
With a weird clarity, he found himself picturing Antonia catching
sight of the piece of paper among his things as he unpacked, picking it up, turning to him questioningly . . . A strange-sounding
laugh escaped from his throat.

He stood motionless, looking out into the gulf of empty space.

THE INCALCULABLE
LIFE GESTURE

Richard Timmerman, principal of an elementary school in the town of Aurelia, noticed a swelling under his chin one morning. Ignoring it (he assumed he was just fighting off some virus), he shaved and went to work. It was still there a week later, but he continued to ignore it. He had a busy job, a family, and plenty of other things to think about.

Among the latter was a problem that had been troubling him for several weeks now. His parents, who had died within months of each other the previous year, had left their house to him and his sister. Ellen, the sister, had moved in with them a few years earlier, ostensibly to help take care of their ailing father, but in reality (as everyone knew who knew the family) because she couldn't afford to buy or rent a place of her own. She had been a reckless spirit when she was young, traveling with a theater troupe in Europe, then living on ashrams in India, and had hit middle age with a crash: twice divorced, with a small son, large debts, and no prospects of making a decent living. Now she was refusing to move out of the house.

It wasn't a big house, but Richard certainly could have used his share of whatever it was worth. He would have hired a lawyer to deal with the matter, but he had qualms about evicting his own sister and was also a little afraid of how this might affect his reputation in the small community where they lived. Being put in this position, of having to be either a victim of Ellen's selfish stubbornness or else a bully, further upset him. Above all, he disliked how the problem, with all the childish feelings it aroused, seemed to have taken over his mind, vexing him whenever he lay in bed or drove to work. Whether he was inwardly fuming at Ellen or trying to force himself to feel more charitable toward her than he did, he could think of nothing else. He considered himself an idealistic person, above this sort of pettiness, but there it was, filling him with its tedious drone every time he had a moment's peace. If she'd had the decency to express guilt or even just some regret about depriving him of what he was owed, he might have found it easier to make allowances for her. But she seemed to think she had every right to stay put and, instead of asking him nicely to be generous or patient, had taken a position of self-righteous hostility, as if he were the one in the wrong. Furthermore, even as she made him feel vaguely criminal for being so much better off than she was (as if siblings somehow had a natural right to equal shares of whatever the world had to offer), she had a way of conveying lofty contempt for precisely the comforts—a decent car, occasional vacations, enough money to shop at the all-organic store in town rather than have to hunt for bargains in the Wal-Mart produce aisles—that distinguished his life from hers. Their phone conversations had become icy in the extreme.

Three weeks after he'd noticed it, the swelling still hadn't gone down. At his wife's urging, he made an appointment to see Dr. Taubman, the family physician, in East Deerfield.

The doctor was a small, trim, dapper man with a neatly shaped goatee and a pair of sparkling half-moon glasses. Largely on the basis of the latter, Richard had formed an idea of him as a person of intellectual leanings, like himself, though also like himself more interested in the nurturing of others (their bodies in his case, while in Richard's it was their young minds) than in the selfish pursuit of learning for its own sake. He felt an affinity with him, and although their conversations had never gone very far, he sensed that an unspoken mutual respect existed between them.

Dr. Taubman picked up a silver pen after examining the lump. He was silent for a moment; then he cleared his throat.

"I don't want to say this is anything like lymphoma," he said, swiveling the pen in his fingers. "It could be perfectly benign, just a swollen lymph node from an infection, as you suggested. But at this point you need to have a specialist take a look at it, and I think you should probably have it removed."

Richard blinked, momentarily too stunned to speak.

"You mean, surgically?" he asked.

"Oh yes."

Smiling oddly, the doctor told Richard to schedule a CAT scan as soon as possible and to make an appointment to see an ear, nose, and throat specialist for a biopsy. As if foreseeing that Richard would attempt to stave off the fear mounting inside him with the hope that these tests might turn out negative, he cautioned him that some tumors were not radiopaque and would therefore not show up on the scan. He added that the specialist would probably opt for surgery regardless of the biopsy results since these also were not entirely reliable.

Recommending a local colleague, he stood up, still smiling and clearly expecting Richard to observe some unwritten clinic protocol in which it was agreed to behave as if a diagnosis of probable cancer were nothing out of the ordinary and certainly nothing to get upset about, at least not in his office. Considering his high regard for the man, Richard couldn't help feeling that he was being dealt with rather brusquely. He stumbled out into the parking lot with a sense of having been sent on his way with an armful of enormous, unwieldy objects that had been pressed on him against his wishes and for which he had no conceivable use.

He had intended running some errands in East Deerfield after the appointment, but he drove home instead, his hands slippery on the cold plastic of the steering wheel.

In the driveway he stood for a moment, feeling dizzy. The white clapboard and blue trim of the house gleamed in the spring sunshine. Beyond, spaced across the broad lawn, were the shade trees that had outlasted several generations of humans: the weeping willow, the giant and festive blue spruce, the sugar maple and horse chestnut standing close to each other, their branches interlaced. All just as he had left them an hour and a half earlier and yet charged with an air of circumspection now, as if the news had already reached them.

Sara, his wife, appeared from around the back of the house in her gardening gloves, her short graying hair clinging in damp wisps to her face.

"What did the doctor say?"

She nodded silently as he told her. A stranger observing might have imagined her oddly unconcerned by the news. But this subdued reaction was simply her manner, the manifestation of a slow but scrupulous way she had of registering important matters. It was she who insisted that Richard go down to New York for both the scan and the biopsy, rather than have them done locally, and it was she, in her unobtrusively efficient way, who made the arrangements.

A week later he took the train to New York and entered a building on the Upper West Side. He had barely slept since his visit to Dr. Taubman. Some over-the-counter pills had given him a few hours of light oblivion each night, after which the feeling of dread they had held in precarious abeyance spilled back, filling his mind with a cold, pulsating wakefulness for the rest of the night. It happened to be a busy week at his school—a meeting with trustees, a planning session for a new science building, the monthly assembly for the "Tribes" program that he had recently introduced—and the effort of trying to conduct himself in his usual genial manner compounded the stress, leaving him with a muffled, torpid, leaden sensation that was somehow at the same time one of weightlessness and raw-nerved exposure.

Utter silence filled the elevator; it seemed not to move at all, so that when the doors opened, it was as if the lobby had merely transformed itself into a corridor with a glass sign etched with the words LIFESTREAM RADIOLOGY.

He went into the waiting room, feeling the fear inside him glow a little brighter. Was it death itself that frightened him? Not exactly. Nonexistence had never seemed a particularly disturbing concept, and he had often wondered why people made such a fuss about it. More upsetting was the prospect of being reassigned in the minds of others from the category of the living to that of the dying, which appeared to him a kind of sudden ruin, an abrupt, calamitous coming down in the world, with all the disgrace and shame that accompany such a circumstance. And then beyond that there was the process, terrifying to contemplate, of being slowly, forcibly, painfully torn from one's own existence. Already, it seemed to him, the process had begun; a fissure had opened between him and the life he had made for himself: the wife and children he loved, the home in which their happiness had flourished, his demanding but inexhaustibly satisfying job. The fissure was still invisible, but like an ice floe that had cracked, it was only a matter of time before the two sides began to move apart.

After twenty minutes his name was called, and he was shown to a room where the radiologist, a woman with straggling gray hair and a wooden cross at her neck, prepared him for the scan.

"I'll be giving you a power surge injection of iodine for radiographic contrast," she said with a strained, bulging-eyed look, "after which you may become nauseous or feel the need for a bowel movement. But it's important that you lie completely still and try not to swallow as that can affect the image."

He hung his head, restraining a childish desire to sob.

"We'll go on in if you're ready . . ."

The walls of the scanning room were windowless, hung with huge, glowing photographic panels depicting sapphire waterfalls and emerald green alpine meadows. In the center stood the monumental white ring of the scanner with the gurney projecting below. From pictures he had seen of these machines, Richard had noted their strange fusion of the space age with the primeval, but even so, the vast size and eerie fluorescence of the instrument startled him. He lay down on the narrow dais. The woman plunged a needle into his arm. A tingling, pressurized heat surged into him. Not painful exactly, but shocking. The word "insult," in its medical sense, came to him as the substance raced through his veins. Something in him seemed to flinch in corresponding outrage or mortification. Was he going to throw up? Were his bowels going to betray him? Two lit faces suspended in darkness watched from behind a glass partition. The scanner began to hum. Above him the radiologist stood with her slight aghast expression, her stringy hair bluish in the light from the machine. She pressed a switch, and the gurney slid his prone body slowly under the machine's arching panel of dials and sensors. By nature a respecter of limits and thresholds, he stared up at the great circular gateway towering over him with a feeling of horror.

He swallowed suddenly, the reflex too strong to control.

"Sorry!"

"It's all right. I think we have what we're looking for."

Before he could fully absorb these words, the woman had re-
treated behind the glass partition, conferring inaudibly with the
two figures stationed there. A few minutes later she reemerged,
carrying a large envelope. The wooden cross gleamed dully at her
throat. She handed him the envelope, speaking slowly: "This is
what you're going to bring with you to your specialist."

He thanked her, putting on his jacket. On his way out he
turned back, hearing himself ask in a thick voice: "Did you—did
you see something?"

She looked away from him, facing the machine.

"Oh, I don't really read the scans."

She had seen something! She was religious, and even a small
lie made her uncomfortable. He left, staggering out into the cool
spring sunlight. The specialist's office was in midtown. He walked,
moving in the same daze of fear as before, only more deeply in-
terred in its cause. Here was Broadway, billboards and scaffolding
and more billboards over the scaffolding. A truck, turning, belched
soot across a pool of white tulips. Why had this happened to him?
he wondered. Had he committed some transgression without knowing it? Violated some fundamental law governing his life? He had
been brought up in a churchgoing household, and although he no
longer believed in a god or an afterlife, the habit of looking for
meaning in the events that befell him was second nature. He carried with him a sense of having discovered at a certain point the
precise terms on which existence was prepared to nourish his particular qualities as a human being, and of having abided by these
terms as conscientiously as he could. He had been interested in
many things: folk music, mathematics, philosophy, design. He had
thought of becoming an academic, another time considered a career in engineering. But always at the point of embarking along
one of these paths some stubborn element in his makeup had pro-

tested that although these professions might be fascinating, they lacked a particular radiance without which his own nature was not going to fulfill itself. This was the radiance of active virtue; direct, self-sacrificing involvement in the upward-aspiring efforts of his fellow humans. How this had become such a vital necessity to him he had not thought necessary to investigate, but there it was, in him like a compass needle, and he had followed it faithfully as it led him into the field of education, guiding him within that field to the progressive theories that articulated his own instincts, pointing the way forward at every juncture in his career . . . Educators, he had read in an essay that had inscribed itself on his memory, were "the life-priests of the new era." They were "adepts"—he knew the passage as he had once known the Nicene Creed—"in the dark mystery of living, fearing nothing but life itself, and subject to nothing but their own reverence for the incalculable life gesture . . ."

The incalculable life gesture . . . And yet here was death growing in his throat! He remembered a visit he and Sara had made to a relative of Sara's in Minneapolis. They had walked down the Nicollet Mall to the river and come to a place called Cancer Survivor's Park. The name, in stenciled metal letters over the gate, had shocked him. Its brazen literalness where some poetic euphemism might have been expected gave its summons to celebrate the afflicted an aggressive thrust that had made him want to do just the opposite: to recoil from the very thought of such ghoulish beings. And yet now his best hope was to become one of them!

"Spare a dollar, mister?"

A panhandler had intruded an empty coffee cup into his field of vision. Richard dropped some change into the cup. The man's eyes went straight to the coins, counting them. He turned away without a word of thanks.

A familiar stung sensation flared in Richard, reminding him
how much he had come to dislike the city. He had found it exhila-
rating in the days when he lived here, but now, increasingly, he felt
himself at odds with it. Every time he came down it seemed harder,
cruder, more mercantile, the people thronging its streets crazier
and more grotesque. On his last visit he had seen a woman in
stiletto heels leading a muzzled raccoon on a leash. He didn't think
of himself as censorious, let alone a prude, but the place seemed to
bring forth some puritanical layer of his personality. A steady
stream of disapproving observations would flow through him, un-
bidden. Even now he found himself grimly taking note of new
depths of folly, new kinds of utterly unnecessary things—gadgets,
clothes, jewelry, services, entertainments—publicized on every
available surface in newly unpleasant ways, the ads caught up in
their own logic of escalating tawdriness. One for a dating website
outside a subway showed a near-naked couple grinning in post-
coital bliss. Two intertwined hearts glowed above them, but it
might just as well have been genitalia. The ideal state of affairs,
things seemed to imply, was a continual orgy. If you weren't desirable, then dye your hair, spend the day in a tanning salon, sign up
at one of these gyms that flaunted their robotic, Lycra-clad members at passersby through vast street-level windows. Turn the
inside of your head into your own private rock stadium . . . The
steady convergence of mainstream commerce with what had once
been marginal or underground was peculiarly dismaying. In the
past, when you grew sick of one of these worlds, you could shift,
mentally, into the other, but now they had consolidated, and there
was nowhere to escape. The whole world, as he had read somewhere, was an underworld. If you described New York to even
a liberal-minded person of fifty years ago, he would tell you the
apocalypse must have come . . .

But in the thick of these thoughts a sudden bewilderment seized him. Where did they come from? What was the basis, within him, for this indignation? On what rock of conviction was it founded? If you didn't believe in God or the soul or the here-after, then what was a human being if not merely living meat? And if that was so, then surely it was natural to want to be healthy, nubile, muscular, lusty . . . Better that than *tainted* meat, as he had become! It was he himself who was grotesque, surely, with this little death kernel growing in his throat.

The specialist's offices were in a grandiose corner building. Granite steps led from the tree-lined street to a revolving door. Behind it was a dim lobby with a uniformed doorman, who sent Richard up to the seventh floor. The offices themselves were sleekly modern, furbished in brushed steel and blond wood. The young woman receptionist was dressed like a model, with a puff of pink chiffon at her throat. There were no files or papers of any kind on her desk. Occasionally she spoke into thin air, answering an invisible, inaudible telephone.

The specialist, a Dr. Jameson, was much younger than Richard had expected: mid-thirties, with thick fair hair and large freckles on his boyish face. Long ginger eyelashes gave him a sleepy, hedonistic look.

"Come on in, Mr., uh, Timmerman," he said, glancing at some papers.

He sat Richard in a contraption like a dentist's chair while he read through the referral papers, apparently for the first time. "Huh," he said neutrally. With a light toss he dropped the papers onto the desk.

"Let's take a look."

He leaned in over Richard, probing with strong, well-manicured fingers into the soft tissue under Richard's chin. He wore a watch that appeared to have neither numerals nor hands, and he smelled faintly of vanilla.

Another laconic "huh" was his only comment after the examination. He stepped back over to the desk and picked up the envelope that Richard had brought, taking out the CAT scan images. He examined them for a long, silent interval.

"This is upstate somewhere, this, uh, East Deerfield?"

"Yes." Richard could hear the tremor in his own voice. Evidently he was about to be advised to move closer to some urban area with access to state-of-the-art treatment facilities. In which case it was all over.

"Why?" he asked.

"No reason. I just . . ."

The doctor yawned.

"Excuse me. Sorry. You have a stone in your saliva gland. A small calcium deposit. Sialolithiasis is the technical term. If it becomes uncomfortable, you can have it removed surgically, maybe broken up with ultrasound. Otherwise it'll probably work its own way out. Either way it's not a big deal."

Richard felt as if he were levitating out of the chair.

"You mean, there's no—there's no lymphoma?"

"No."

Only as he took the elevator back down did he pick up the note of faint scorn in the question about East Deerfield, the amused disdain of the cosmopolitan practitioner for his colleague out in the sticks. A smile rose on his lips. With it, clarified by the strong joy of the moment, came the memory of his obscure sense of having been too hastily dismissed by Dr. Taubman, as if the man had been afraid he was going to start visibly decaying right there in his office and scare away the other patients. He would have liked to strut into Taubman's office, not so much to berate him for his mistake as to flaunt his freshly certified health in the man's face . . .

It was still sunny outside. He walked slowly toward the train station, conscious of how rare it was to be able to savor, so undistractedly, the pure pleasure of being alive. Everything he looked at, every face he passed, seemed a part of this pleasure, a fiery splendor suffusing even the most mundane things. A deliveryman bustled by, wheeling stacks of clear-topped containers in which the vivid colors of cold cuts and raw vegetables, each partitioned in their own segment, glowed—it seemed to Richard—like the panels of a rose window in some ancient cathedral. In a parking lot behind a row of blossoming trees a shiny crimson car was being lifted effortlessly into the air by a hydraulic steel arm. Glorious! As he passed by, Richard realized he hadn't thought of his quarrel with his sister for days; not since his visit to Dr. Taubman. How trivial that whole business seemed. How absurd to have let it upset him as much as it had. In his exhilarated state the solution appeared obvious: he must call Ellen right away, tell her she could stay in the house for as long as she wanted. In his heart of hearts he had always known this was the right thing to do; he simply hadn't been able to summon, with any conviction, the feeling of largesse such a gesture would require. Now, however, he felt it in abundance. True, he had been counting on his share of the sale to put something substantial aside for his children's college fund, perhaps also build a screened-in porch so that they could eat outside in summer. But so what? He had a life—in every sense!— whereas Ellen had nothing. If it meant so much to her to go on living in the family home, then let her. Let her! The decision further boosted his sense of euphoria. As he took out his phone, he seemed to glimpse some large, resplendent state of existence opening itself up to him.

He dialed her number.

"What?" came the familiar voice.

"Ellen, it's me, Richard."

"I know. What do you want?"

"I just—" He broke off. Her hostile tone, though no different from the usual way she'd been talking to him since their quarrel began, presented an unexpected obstacle. It seemed necessary to bring her into his exuberant state of mind before he could reveal his momentous decision.

"I'm in New York. Our doctor thought I had lymphoma because of a lump under my chin, and I've spent the last week thinking I was going to die. But I'm not. I've just come out of a specialist's office, and he says I'm fine. It was just a stone!"

He paused. Ellen said nothing.

"I thought I'd call you, you know . . ." He trailed off, unnerved by the silence at the other end.

"I see," she said finally. "Well, I'm happy for you, Richard. I'm glad you're not going to die. But now I'm afraid I have to go out. Since my car's broken down again, Scott and I have to start walking to the post office so I can pay my bills before it closes. Otherwise I'm sure I'd have time to chat."

The martyred tone was a specialty of hers. He tried not to let it provoke him.

"Listen. Ellen. I want to talk about the house."

"Ah. I thought so."

God, she was impossible! She knew him well enough to have an idea where he was trying to go with this. But was she going to be gracious about it? No! She was going to make it as unpleasant as possible. Already he could feel the old rankling annoyance mounting inside him. How easy it would be to succumb: lash out at her for making others pay the price for her hapless way of living, present her with some stark, inflexible ultimatum . . . But he resisted it. He was damned if he was going to let her stop him making his great gesture of magnanimity. He would do it for his own sake, if not hers.

"What I want to tell you," he said, forcing out the words, "is that I've decided to let you stay on in the house for as long as you need to. That's all."

There was a long pause.

"Well, that's awfully charitable of you, Richard, and I'm glad you won't be trying to have me and Scott evicted from our home. But since I had no intention of leaving anyway, it doesn't really change anything, does it? Now if it's okay with you, I have to run."

She hung up.

He moved on down Seventh Avenue, stunned. He told himself that he'd said what he wanted to say, and that was all that mattered; that however she took it, he'd acquitted himself with dignity and compassion. Furthermore, he'd brought an end to their tedious, unseemly quarrel, and now, finally, he would be able to turn his mind to loftier things again.

But all the earlier expansiveness had gone from him; in its place a drab, ashen sensation, as if the bitterness of his sister's dismal existence had flowed into him through the phone.

And for a moment he felt as if he hadn't yet had his appointment with Dr. Jameson after all; as if he were still waiting, frightened and uncertain, for his diagnosis.

The Half Sister

The house was a square Victorian building with a white stuccoed facade and balustraded balconies at the windows. Twelve granite steps, sheltered by a glass-paned awning, led up to a massive front door with a brass lion's head glaring from its center.

On Tuesday afternoons at five o'clock Martin Sefton would climb the steps to give the Knowles boys their weekly lessons on the classical guitar. An au pair would let him in. Passing through a hallway that smelled of floor polish and fresh flowers, he would carry his guitar up the four flights of stairs to the boys' rooms at the top of the house. As he climbed, he could see out of the landing windows onto the back garden, and sometimes he would pause to look down at the sizable lawn surrounded by a mass of blossoms and foliage.

It was in a garden very like this that Martin had been inspired, at the age of twelve, to become a classical guitarist. The occasion had been a summer party in Highgate, where a man in a psychedelic shirt had been playing flamboyant pieces on his honey-colored instrument out on the grass, surrounded by beautiful, spellbound women. A distant, somewhat rueful memory of the event would echo through Martin as he gazed down at the Knowleses' garden. Despite his having studied diligently at the Royal College, where he had been encouraged by his teachers to hope for great things, his career as a performer had not taken off. By the time he accepted that it wasn't going to, his energies, as far as any large ambition was concerned, had been fully consumed. Besides, there was nothing else he wanted to do.

After he had given the boys their lessons, he would make his way back downstairs, where an envelope would be waiting for him on the bowlegged hall table, with a check inside, signed by Mrs. Knowles. Like her two sons, Mrs. Knowles was dark-haired and pale-skinned with bright blue eyes and the kind of delicately faceted English features that can arouse feelings of vague inferiority in those, like Martin, who do not possess them. She cultivated an extreme refinement of appearance that had made her seem momentarily older than her years when Martin met her on his first visit to the house. She had been arranging flowers in the vase on the hall table when he arrived and had continued doing so as she spoke to him, barely glancing in his direction after an initial, coolly appraising smile of welcome. Since then Martin had seen her only once, standing in a corridor speaking on a cordless phone, a secretive smile at her lips. She was wearing pink nail polish, pearl earrings, and a white silk T-shirt, under which her breasts showed like two thorns. Martin had nodded at her, but although she was looking directly at him, she gave no indication of seeing him.

One afternoon, a few months after Martin had started teaching, a large man strode out from a corridor to waylay him on the stairs.

"Hello there, I'm John Knowles. Good to meet you at last." The man shook Martin's hand warmly, treating him to an undisguised once-over. "How are the boys coming along?"

"Pretty well, I think."

"Good. Smashing."

The man stood very close to him. His voice was powerful, not booming, but imposing enough to make Martin feel that he himself was mumbling. There was the residue of a Midlands accent in his speech. He must have been in his fifties, solidly built, with silvering eyebrows and thickets of dark hair in his nostrils and ears. He began questioning Martin about his life, affably and in some detail, though at the same time showing little apparent interest in the answers themselves. "Good, good," he said briskly after each one, then impatiently shifted the line of inquiry. Where had Martin studied? Were his parents still alive? Which part of London did he live in?

"And your own career . . . giving concerts and . . . such"—he gestured at the guitar case in Martin's hand—"going all right, is it?"

"Not bad, thank you," Martin replied circumspectly. The understanding, or at least the agreed-on pretense, with the people who paid him to teach their offspring was that they were supporting a struggling artist, not just hiring some hack.

"Good, good. Hard work, I should imagine, making a name for yourself in that field."

"Not easy."

"Right. The world's full of bloody virtuosos! But no wife and children to support, at least. Or perhaps you do have?" The man's yellowish gray eyes settled for a moment on Martin's, forceful but also uneasy-looking, as though he half expected to be told to mind his own business.

"No."

"There you go. Something to be grateful for, eh?" He gave a blustering laugh, to which Martin responded with a polite smile.

"Well, stop and have a drink with us one night after you've finished with the boys, will you?"

"All right. Thanks."

Two weeks later Martin was accosted by the man again:

"That drink I mentioned . . . how would tonight work for you?"

Martin hesitated. He preferred not to socialize with his employers. The less he was obliged to say about himself in his capacity as a musician, the better. Not that he wasn't reconciled with the state of things in that side of his life; he just didn't enjoy feigning enthusiasm for something that was now simply a way of paying the rent. He looked for a harmless way of declining, but under the peculiarly overbearing nature of Mr. Knowles's presence—its odd mixture of assertiveness and unctuousness—his mind had gone blank.

"That sounds pleasant," he heard himself say as the moment for plausible excuses passed. "Thank you."

"Good, good. We'll see you later then. Just family. Tristan'll show you down."

At six-thirty the older boy escorted Martin down to a large living room on the ground floor, softly lit, with silk-striped wallpaper and a pair of French windows opening onto the garden. Mrs. Knowles was on a sofa next to her younger son. Her dark hair was up in braided coils with a few tendrils falling about her small ears. An intricate mesh of sapphires, the same blue as her eyes, circled the skin above the neckline of an evening dress.

"It's nice of you to join us," she said. "Tristan, run and tell Daddy our guest is here." She smiled distantly at Martin. "My husband'll get you a drink, in just a moment." She turned to her younger son, ruffling his hair and fussing with his collar. Martin registered her apparent indifference to himself. At one time such behavior might have offended him, but now he couldn't have cared less. He observed her dispassionately. Her particular haughty beauty reminded him of a painting he had seen at an impressionable age, a portrait of an aristocratic lady carrying an enormous muff and striding across fields under a wild dark sky, her elaborate coiffure disheveled by the wind; her expression, at once hard and avid, provocatively suggestive of a woman on her way to an assignation. His eye was drawn to the sapphires, which rose from the pale flesh below her neck like some crystalline outcropping of her blue blood. Seeing Martin glance at them, she brought her hand up to her throat—almost defensively, it seemed, though she appeared surprised to find them there.

"Oh. We're going on to a dinner at the Nigerian Embassy. John's building a dam outside Lagos."

"Ah."

"That's why I'm all dressed up."

Martin smiled, wondering if this was meant to convey that she wasn't all dressed up for him and noting that not even an outright put-down, if that was what this was, had the power to touch him anymore. His ability to detach himself from a situation in this way was a source of satisfaction to him, though he did sometimes wonder where, to what state of glacial impermeability, it was leading.

Mr. Knowles strode into the room, pink cheeked from shaving and decked out in black tie. With him came a large, strange-looking woman of twenty-five or so, in a shapeless brown dress.

"There you are," he said. "Sorry to keep you. What'll it be?"

Martin asked for a gin and tonic.

"By the way, this is my daughter, Charmian, the boys' half sister."

Martin nodded at the woman. She murmured a greeting and sat on a hard chair at the edge of the room, staring forward with an expression that looked like fear, but was probably just the effect of her eyes being unnaturally prominent and far apart. Mrs. Knowles gave her a faint smile, from which she seemed to cringe. She was painfully unattractive.

"Charmian's off in Devon most of the time," her father said, "learning to be a horticulturist or some such thing. But occasionally we're graced with a visit. Whiskey, you said?"

"Gin and tonic."

"Right you are. Tell him about the gardening, love. She works like a slave for this landscape gardening company. Everything from potting the azaleas to digging bloody great ditches with a bulldozer, and all for next to nothing, which seems to me a bit daft considering she could buy the company ten times over with what we've given her, but there it is, wants to work her way up the hard way. Not that I'm against that, mind you . . ."

The girl's face grew steadily pinker as her father spoke. She twisted a lock of her lank, mousy hair, her eyes bulging and blinking. There was an aura of debilitation about her, as though she had fought hard but been crushingly defeated in the side of life having to do with appearances and social graces. One of her eyes, Martin suddenly noticed, was dead, the light out in its gray iris. He looked away, sipping his drink and wondering how soon he could leave.

Mr. Knowles came to an end, and as the girl said nothing, Martin felt it was his turn to make a contribution, if only to show he wasn't completely lacking in the social graces himself. He turned to Mrs. Knowles.

"Nice garden you've got out there, speaking of gardens."

"Thank you. We enjoy it."

"That's one thing I miss where I live, a garden."

"I know what you mean. They can make such a difference."

"I first got the idea of becoming a guitarist in a garden like that."

He hadn't known he was going to say that when he embarked on the topic, but the thought that he was now going to impose an intimate personal anecdote on Mrs. Knowles filled him with a cer-

tain malicious glee. He realized that he had, after all, been stung
by her offhand manner.

"Oh?" Mrs. Knowles adjusted her posture warily on the sofa.
Her lips bunched together, little dimples of polite anticipatory
amusement forming on either side of them. Assuming a tone of
light self-mockery, Martin began to describe the party he had gone
to as a boy. At first he felt poised and fluent, so much so that he
found himself half imagining he was a fellow guest at the embassy
dinner Mrs. Knowles had said she was going on to, some suave
diplomat seated next to her and mesmerizing her with his stories,
and in the briefly cushioning sweetness of this fantasy, he allowed
himself to acknowledge that this disdainful woman—younger
than himself, he realized—had stirred vague desires in him. For
a minute or two he became expansive, flippantly evoking the little vision of combined hedonism and virtuosity he had received in
that other garden. But as he did so, he felt an unexpected pang go
through him, as though the event still held a charge of its original
brilliance and had released it in a sudden vengeful throb. Jarred,
he felt his tone falter. Then to his dismay, he lost his way in the anecdote, trailing off on an unintended and rather mawkish note of
self-pity. Mrs. Knowles looked at him for a moment, saying nothing, but leaving him in no doubt that he had humiliated himself.

All the while he had been aware of the half sister listening to
him intently. He glanced at her now. His story appeared to have
touched some chord in her; her face was a study in anguished sympathy. On second thoughts he wasn't so sure that the eye was
dead—maybe just askew in its socket or lazy. He felt uncomfortably transparent under her gaze. She seemed on the point of saying something to him. He turned brusquely away.

"So you like the outdoors then?" he heard Mr. Knowles say.
"Plants and trees and all that?"

"Well . . . I suppose so."

"Just like Charmian! She's always been a great one for the out-doors, haven't you, love? We're thinking of buying her a house with some land that's come up for sale near our cottage. Somewhere she can run her landscaping business from when she's ready . . ."

"Oh . . ."

"Yes, stonking great piece of land actually. Almost a hundred acres. In Dorset, near the sea. Do you like the sea?"

"Yes."

"Well, it's just five minutes away. Gorgeous. I don't know if you're familiar with that coast, but for my money it beats any-where on the bloody Mediterranean . . ."

So it continued for another half hour. Then Mrs. Knowles looked ostentatiously at her watch, and a moment later, to his re-lief, Martin was in the hallway, saying goodbye.

Mr. Knowles gripped his hand. "By the way," he said, "are you doing anything special tomorrow evening?"

"I'm not sure . . . I'll have to . . ."

"Just that we have tickets for Covent Garden. *Peter Grimes*, isn't it, dearest?"

Mrs. Knowles nodded. "Rather good seats, I believe."

"Unfortunately it turns out we can't go." Mr. Knowles contin-ued. "Might you be interested?"

Martin loathed opera himself, but there was a woman he had met recently, a dancer working at the health food restaurant where he sometimes ate, who might be impressed by an invitation to Covent Garden. He hesitated.

"We'd been looking forward to going"—Mr. Knowles pressed on—"but I have a client in from Dubai just for the one night, and he wants to have dinner at one of these celeb chef places instead, so there it is. What do you say?"

Rebecca, the woman's name was, slim and tall with pillowy red lips and no rings in her nose or eyebrows. They'd been sizing each

other up for a couple of weeks, flirting casually. He'd been thinking it was getting time to make a more definite move.

"Well," he said cautiously, "if you're sure . . ."

"Now I know Charmian's keen on going, aren't you, love?
Which is one ticket taken care of. And since neither of the boys can
be persuaded, we thought you might like the other one. I imagine
you would, as a music lover?"

Martin gaped at Mr. Knowles, absorbing this. The full extent
and depth of the man's wheedling, coercive personality seemed to
have suddenly disclosed itself, like some strange creature opening
unsuspected wings. He realized he had been maneuvered into a
position where he had no choice but to agree to accompany the girl
to the opera. As he heard himself do so, he was aware of Mrs.
Knowles walking serenely out of the hall with an air of having
seen all she cared to of something a little unseemly, of the two
boys looking at their father and him with expressions of neutral
appraisal, and of their half sister, Charmian, standing with her
head bowed under what seemed an incapacitating weight of mor-
tified shame, her large hands gripping the lavish scroll at the end
of the banister as if for support.

"Grand. That's settled then," Mr. Knowles was saying. "We'll
see you here around six tomorrow evening, shall we?"

"All right," Martin said, angrily telling himself that as soon as
he got home, he would phone back with some excuse.

As he was turning to go, the girl looked up at him. "You don't
have to come if you don't want to." Her voice was low and surprisingly melodious.

"Now what's that about, girl?" her father demanded, frowning. "The man's just said he wants to come!"

"I mean, if for some reason you discover you can't come after
all, I won't mind."

Martin held her gaze a moment. Her face was really very strange—large and oval, with a propitiatory quality, like a salver on which certain curious, unrelated objects were being offered up for inspection.

"I'm sure there won't be any problem," he muttered. "I'll see you tomorrow."

He sensed immediately that she knew he was lying. Once again he felt utterly exposed, as though she could see not only through this small deceit but all the way inside him, past his stoicism, past the disappointments underneath, and on into whatever mysterious flaw had brought them about in the first place. And far from accusatory, she seemed oddly forgiving, her expression suggestive of inexhaustible, pent-up sympathies. He turned abruptly and left.

On the bus home he concocted a story about having to visit a sick aunt in Surrey a day earlier than he'd thought. That would do for an excuse. What the hell did they think? That he was going to pretend to fall for the girl? All this time, he realized with a flare of rage, he had been under discreet scrutiny as he'd made his way up and down through the quiet house, had been appraised and judged suitable (suitably modest in his aspirations, was it, or just suitably hard-up and opportunistic?) as a candidate for what had no doubt been a long-standing attempt on the part of the household to off-load its damaged goods. The image of her sorrowful face came into his mind. "You don't have to come if you don't want to," he heard her say again in her gentle voice. He turned his head abruptly.

Out through the windows he watched the glazed cornucopias of the Fulham Road reel by, then the river, bronze with red ripples in the July dusk. Another fantasy, half vengeful, half erotic, played itself out in his mind: he imagined himself marrying Charmian, living with her in a big house in the country. On weekends, while she potted azaleas or worked a bulldozer somewhere, Mrs. Knowles would run across the fields to him in her finery, while he waited for her in some dark barn or stable. He pictured her in a state of reluctant subjection to her own desires, undressing for him, offering him her sharp breasts. Then the image of Charmian's face loomed back: large, sad, beseeching, full of forgiveness . . . A wry look turned his lips; she, at least, knew what was what. Too bad she wasn't prettier. In another world you might find happiness with a girl like that, but not this. Not him. Again he looked out, trying to rid himself of her image. The ocher brick semis and tatty high-rises of his part of London appeared. He liked the area, its anonymity and total lack of pretension. As soon as he got home, he would phone the Knowleses with his excuse. Then what? Go to the health food restaurant perhaps, have his usual tempeh and rice up at the mosaic counter, chatting with Rebecca. Maybe he'd suggest a drink after her shift. She'd look at him a moment, resting her eyes on his, long enough to convey that she understood what he was asking, then purse her pillowy lips and say either yes or no. If yes, they'd have a couple of drinks at the after-hours bar by the tube station, then either that night or the next go back to his place. Before they fell into bed, he'd take out his guitar and play her a couple of his party pieces: the Bach Sarabande; a minuet by Sor. The affair might last a few weeks, maybe a couple of months. Then all the usual crap would start: other lovers creeping out of the woodwork, insufferable best friends, incompatible habits and needs, problems that nothing short of falling seriously in love could solve, and having given up on the idea of becoming a husband and father in any style he could have tolerated, Martin had disciplined himself not to fall in love some time ago. This was the pattern of his life. He had no desire to change it and no intention of letting anyone else change it for him.

All the while the half sister's strange face continued hovering in his mind's eye, gazing at him with its look of unasked-for sympathy. Again he heard her voice: "You don't have to come if you don't want to." He shook his head violently. "Too bloody right I don't," he muttered as he got off the bus. The people getting on stared at him, but he didn't notice. He was in the thick of a battle, and it seemed to him he needed every ounce of his strength to defend himself.

THE OLD MAN

The two women appeared in Conrad's office late one afternoon in March. Olga, the mother, had rouged cheeks wrinkled like walnut shells and wore several rings on her gnarled fingers. The daughter was blond, with a flat, handsome face and a full figure that she carried with confidence. According to her résumé, she was thirty-eight years old. Her name was Lydia Krasnova.

The two had come from the former Czechoslovakia, where they had worked in a flower-growing cooperative until the fall of communism. After making their way to the States, they had settled in Albany, opening a flower stand near the Rensselaer train station with the help of a loan from an émigré business fund. From there they'd scoured the area for a plot of land where they could start their own growing business. They'd found a two-acre lot a few miles outside the city. There was a house on the property, which they'd moved into, and a dilapidated cottage, which they rented out. Now they were looking for some capital to start building the greenhouses.

The mother, who spoke little English, eyed Conrad silently while Lydia did the talking. The presentation was polished and thorough. They had priced heaters, ventilation systems, and sprinklers; found suppliers for soil additives and fertilizers; talked to dis-

tributors; and set up preliminary agreements with wholesalers in
New York.

Conrad listened without interrupting. At the end he told the
women he needed to make some calculations of his own, but he
knew already that he was going to give them the small sum they
were asking for. He had had more than two decades of experience
in the kind of small business venture they were describing, and he
had an instinct for a sound proposition.

On their way out the mother pointed a bony finger at the
framed photograph on his desk. "Your daughter?"

"No. That's my wife."

"Young!"

"Well . . . She died. Nine years ago."

"Oh! I . . . Sorry . . ."

"That's okay."

The old woman looked helplessly at her daughter. In an easy
gesture Lydia turned back and looked at the photograph, placing
her hand on the desk next to the frame.

"You must miss her," she said.

"I do."

"What was her name?"

"Margot."

"She's pretty."

"Thank you."

They left. In the quiet room Conrad looked out through the
window. A cement barge was gliding down the river in the evening
light. It moved slowly, almost too slowly for Conrad to gauge any
movement at all, but he watched until it disappeared.

————

Preparation of the site began that summer. On Conrad's first
visit Lydia and her mother were in rubber boots, overseeing the

clearing of the trees. The logging crew had cut down a thick stand of hardwoods and were dragging the stumps out of the dirt. Chaos of one kind or another always prevailed at the beginning of a new project, and this was no different except perhaps in its raw physicality and the fact that these two women, one so bent and ancient, the other so immaculately elegant, were its source. The place was cratered like a bomb site, with huge, mutilated trunks lying in piles, great tangles of upturned roots that seemed to writhe in the light, and a powerful, almost animal smell of sap in the air. The wood was going to be sold at the lumberyard, and the women, who seemed to know about such things, were instructing the loggers to hide flaws in the trunks by roughing the surface with the toothed edge of the backhoe's metal bucket.

"More! More!" the old woman screeched at the driver over the roar and clank of the huge machine. "Good! Stop!"

A week later bulldozers leveled the dirt, and soon after that the contractor brought in the steel and glass for the houses themselves. Tunnel frames with plastic sheeting would have been cheaper to build but harder to heat in winter, and in this, as in all other aspects of the project, the women had persuaded Conrad that the higher-priced option was the only one that could possibly merit serious consideration. There was something lofty, almost aristocratic about these women, Conrad thought, and he found that he approved of this. Lydia, with her queenly bearing and calm practicality, had begun to fascinate him.

They liked to play bridge, and on discovering that Conrad knew the rudiments of the game, they invited him to join them, summoning for a fourth the tenant they had installed in the small cottage next to their house.

This was an old man with little startled red-rimmed eyes and wisps of white hair standing upright as though he'd seen a ghost.

His name was Mirek, and he too was Czech, a distant relative of theirs, who had managed to emigrate in the sixties and lived in Brooklyn, running a used book business until a few years ago, when the lease on his tiny store expired. When Olga and Lydia had looked him up, he was doing menial jobs for a coin and stamp dealer in Manhattan. He had complained so bitterly of the difficulty of keeping body and soul together in the city that later, when the time came for the women to find a tenant for the one-room cottage on their new property, they had decided to ask Mirek if he would like to move there himself. At first he had refused, even less certain of how he would make a living outside the city than inside. But in quick succession two things had happened to change his mind: he had been mugged on the subway, and then the dealer he was working for had moved to Florida. And so he had decided to take his chances with the women. The only job he had found so far was bagging groceries at a Grand Union two miles away, but he seemed cheerful and optimistic about his prospects.

All this came out over the course of several evenings as the bridge games developed into regular weekly events. The four of them sat at a card table in the front room, which had been furnished in an ornate, old-fashioned style, with net curtains, gold-striped wallpaper, and a crimson plush sofa with lace antimacassars. The stakes were small, though the mother saw to it that debts were paid promptly, and she kept a tin box full of change for the purpose. Conrad and the old man partnered each other, and as they almost always lost, a rueful bond established itself between them, and they were able to make up for the sometimes awkward fact of their being barely able to understand a word each other said by an ongoing pantomime of commiserative gestures—sighs, grimaces, outstretched hands.

After the game coffee would be served; then Olga would gather up the cups and withdraw to the kitchen, which would be the old man's cue to leave. Conrad and Lydia would linger on in the front room, talking together with growing comfort and familiarity.

One evening after Mirek had gone home and Olga had disappeared off to the kitchen, the two of them found themselves sitting together in an unusually charged silence. What was there to say? They knew as much about each other as conversation could reveal. Conrad had told her all about his past: growing up in Troy the son of an appliance dealer and an assistant school principal, his steady luck as an investor in local businesses, the feelings he still had for his wife, the brief relationships with other women he had had since her death, the unaccountable tension between him and his daughter, eleven years old when her mother had died and now studying some subject he had never heard of at a college two thousand miles away. For her part Lydia had talked dispassionately about her impoverished childhood; her alcoholic father, who had died when she was young; her ex-husband, a former party official who had punched her in the stomach when she was pregnant, causing her to miscarry. These things she had described in a deliberately detached manner, with faint disgust, as if her father's decline and the behavior of her husband were subjects that offended her because they reflected badly on herself. A woman of her worth, she seemed to imply, ought to have done better than this with the men in her life.

All of which had made a strong impression on Conrad. The thought of this attractive, intelligent woman, whom nature had clearly designed for a life of luxury and ease, living under such circumstances had awakened a protective instinct in him, while her lack of self-pity filled him with admiration.

Looking at her in silence now under the warm light of the pink-shaded lamps, her eyes resting candidly and unflinchingly on his own, he felt bewitched and at a loss for words. With every second the silence seemed to move them more deeply into a place of mysterious communion. It was Lydia who spoke.

"Why don't you show me your house? We've never been there."

"Now?"

"It isn't far . . ."

"All right. I will."

He drove her into Albany, her presence beside him registering itself as a bright vibrancy, the source of some new power that seemed to be surging into his life, driving out the heavy loneliness that had hung inside him like some gray immovable cloud since his bereavement.

The house was on a quiet street in one of the older parts of the city. Lydia took his arm as they climbed to the front door. She stepped inside ahead of him, walking slowly through the down-stairs rooms while he switched on lights behind her. The place was clean and orderly, furnished simply in Margot's taste: a few prim-itives and Federal-era antiques; a porcelain washstand with enamel jugs and bowls; arrangements of dried flowers that she and their daughter used to make, from which all but the last ghost of color had faded.

Lydia turned to him with a smile. "You haven't changed any-thing, have you?"

"Since Margot? I guess not."

"Do you feel strange bringing me here?"

"I don't know. Maybe a little."

"I would feel a little strange."

She moved on, climbing the stairs past the utility rooms on the first landing and on up the next flight, looking into the room Mar-got had used as a study, the daughter's old bedroom, an upstairs parlor with a tiled Dutch stove, Conrad turning on the lights as she moved from room to room. At the threshold of the bedroom that he and Margot had shared he held Lydia back and placed a kiss on her lips. As she moved softly against him, he felt that he had been favored by fortune with a piece of extraordinary luck. He was not a gregarious man, certainly not the type who found it easy to strike up new relationships. The few women of his acquaintance who had flung themselves at him after Margot's death had not attracted him, and despite a few brief affairs, he had begun to suspect he was too old or too uninteresting for the ones who did. He had his businesses to occupy him—shares in a carpet warehouse, interests in a chain of Laundromats and a storage rental company—and there were couples from the days of his marriage who still invited him to join them for dinner. But he had come to think of his life as a man, a member of the male sex, as essentially over. Now, however, as Lydia responded to his embrace in the doorway with tender, uncomplicated warmth, he sensed the possibility of this life beginning again, keen as ever, perhaps even richer for its shadows of loss and grief, and as he drew her across the threshold into the bedroom, a feeling of great joy came into him.

They entered then on a phase of rapidly deepening intimacy. Was this possible, at the age of fifty, to have desire suddenly running through your days like a torrent from some underground spring? Such things apparently had a life and logic of their own. Before long every trace of reserve had vanished from their lovemaking. No woman Conrad had known before, not even Margot, seemed quite so sheerly, so poignantly naked as Lydia when she undressed, and none had ever come to his bed with such open delight. The effect on Conrad was intoxicating. He walked into his office each morning feeling as though he had spent the night drinking at the fountain of youth. That winter he proposed and was accepted with an unhesitating serenity that seemed to confirm his feeling of a deep judiciousness in the prospect of their union, a convergence with the forces of destiny.

Meanwhile the greenhouses were finished: four in a row, the

clean panes of glass glittering in the steel frames of their walls and pitched roofs. A Mexican foreman had been hired, and he and his workers had planted several hundred shrubs in the carefully prepared soil. There was a gravel courtyard out front with a fountain in it that sent up thick, petal-shaped curves of water from a granite bowl. At night the water was lit from below with a powerful crimson light. The women had seen such a fountain at one of the greenhouse operations they had visited in the course of planning their own and had resolved to build one just like it. Now, as you approached the house along the winding county road after dark, you saw first the reddish gold glow of the night growing lights illuminating the sky above the treetops, then the sparkling, light-filled glass of the greenhouses themselves, with the fountain in front shimmering like an enormous, glowing rose.

There was some discussion about where they would all live after the wedding, which was set for the following April. Conrad had assumed that Lydia and her mother would want to move into his house, which was larger and grander than theirs, but they wouldn't hear of moving away from their greenhouses.

"No, no. Not move," the old woman said, wagging her finger at him as though he had threatened her with forcible transfer.

"You move here, my darling," Lydia said. "We'll build an addition if you like."

Her firmness surprised him, but the more he considered it, the more reasonable it seemed. He had given no thought, he realized, to any awkwardness Lydia might feel moving into the house he had shared with Margot. Spending nights there as his lover was one thing, but living there as his wife was no doubt a less enticing prospect. It came to him that if he was to make a go of this new life, he needed a clean break from all the old trappings of his life with Margot. He would sell the house, he decided, auction off the antiques, get rid of all those dusty wreaths and garlands. The decision—he was driving to work as he made it—sent a strange, vertiginous excitement through him. He sped forward, pressing the accelerator as though to drown out any doubt or resistance inside him. A few minutes later, entering his office, he picked up the framed photograph of Margot. She was standing on the balcony of a hotel in Costa Rica: smiling, her dark hair tumbling in the sunshine, blue flowers trailing from the wrought iron bars either side of her. It was shortly after they had returned from this vacation that she had been diagnosed with pancreatic cancer, and she had died later that year. With an abrupt, almost violent gesture, he thrust the photograph, frame and all, into a padded envelope, and carried it down to the storage locker he rented in the basement, where he placed it in a cupboard filled with old contracts and prospectuses. Back upstairs he stood at the window, astonished at what he had done but telling himself that the agitation inside him would soon pass. He had loved Margot and he had grieved for her but a new day was dawning and it seemed to him that Margot herself would have wanted him to rise up and seize it.

———

Beth, his daughter, flew in a few days before the wedding. Though Conrad looked forward to the girl's visits, he always began to feel anxious as the time for them approached. The truth was her presence unnerved him; she had turned into a guarded, watchful young woman, with a way of deploying silences that made him feel as if he were constantly being judged and found lacking. He was pleased that she had agreed to come for the wedding, but the thought of her casting her sardonic eye over Lydia and her mother made him nervous.

The meeting was arranged to take place at a dinner two nights before the ceremony, at Lydia and her mother's house.

They set off at dusk. It was a damp evening, with drifts of

spring moisture in the air. Over the treetops a quarter mile from
the house, the glow of the growing lights appeared, deeper than
usual, it seemed, as though intensified by the mist. As always the
sight aroused a kind of reflexive gladness in Conrad, an answering
glow. Here was the fountain, sending up its crimson-lit curves of
water like tongues of shiny lava. There were the greenhouses, four
fiery crystals rising from the earth, the rose shrubs inside them
bathed in gold light. The place seemed to Conrad more mysteriously resplendent than ever, as though some otherworldly force
were radiating through it. Even Beth looked impressed as they got
out of the car, though she said nothing.

Lydia greeted them at the front door. She took Beth's hands in
hers, kissing her on both cheeks and hugging her warmly. "I'm so
happy to meet you at last!"

They went through to the living room, which was filled with
the smell of roasting meat. Olga came out from the adjoining
kitchen: her wrinkled face rouged and lipsticked, a black Gypsy
skirt under her apron, bordered with garish, angular flowers. She
parked her bent frame in front of Beth, staring at her for a moment.

"Do you like champagne?" she brayed.

"Uh . . . Sure."

"I bring bottle."

She shuffled back into the kitchen, and the three of them sat,
Lydia taking charge of Beth with an easy imperiousness. The girl
seemed subdued, possibly even a little dazzled, Conrad thought, by
the poise and elegance of his bride. Given her usual quickness to
assume a posture of contempt, this seemed an encouraging sign.
Clasping her hand, Lydia launched into an amused account of all
the things that were threatening to go wrong with the upcoming
festivities. The two heated marquees had not yet arrived; the ice
sculptor wasn't returning phone calls; the caterer was reneging on
a promise to supply fresh carp . . .

Olga came back in carrying a tray with the champagne and four glasses.

"Please open for me," she said to Conrad. As he stood to take the bottle, he saw through the kitchen window that the lights were on in Mirek's little cottage at the back of the house. Between the wedding preparations and the distractions of the romance itself, the bridge games had had to be abandoned, and several weeks had passed since Conrad had seen or heard anything of the old man.

"How's Mirek?" he asked, tearing the foil from the bottle. "Shouldn't we invite him over sometime?"

There was a silence.

"Mirek?" Lydia said, frowning. "I didn't tell you?"

"No?"

"He's gone."

Conrad, who had begun untwisting the wire from the cork, stopped.

"What do you mean?"

"He's gone. We had to get rid of him."

"What happened?"

Lydia turned away. "Ask Mother."

He looked to the mother, whose orange lips had bunched up in a grimace.

"Three month!" She spit out the words. "Three month he pay no rent. Nothing! I tell him, 'Mirek, you must pay rent.' He bring me twenty dollars. Twenty! Next month again nothing!"

Conrad resumed untwisting the wire. He could feel his daughter looking at him, and it seemed to him suddenly necessary to act as if nothing out of the ordinary had been said.

"What about his job?" he asked, feigning a purely casual interest.

The old woman threw up her hands in a gesture of violent exasperation.

Lydia answered: "He stopped going. He hurt his knee, and then it was too far for him to walk."

"He couldn't drive?"

"He didn't want to drive. I offered to teach him when he first came."

"He did not want to work!" the old woman interjected.

Very carefully, Conrad removed the wire cage from the cork.

"So . . . where did he go?"

"I don't know, darling," Lydia said. "Back to New York, I suppose. Anyway, I left him at the train station. Why do you want to know?"

"I'm just . . . interested."

"Should we have let him stay without paying?"

"Of course not!"

He looked at her, taking care to avoid his daughter's eye, though he could sense the familiar sardonic light already glittering there.

"Well then . . ." Lydia said, smiling at him. She had put her hair up and was wearing a pale cashmere sweater that clung to her body in softly gleaming curves. Her features in the dim lamplight had an almost Asiatic quality: greenish brown eyes tilting upward at their outer corners, her lips full at the center but vanishing quickly into the curling shadows of two small but luxuriant dimples. She looked ravishing, Conrad thought, confused by the apprehension surging inside him, and she was gazing at him with an expression of pure love.

"Anyway," she continued, "it worked out for the best. We were able to put Fernando in there, with his wife and their little boy. They were living with another family in a two-room apartment in Troy . . ."

Fernando was the foreman they had hired for the greenhouses.

"I see," Conrad said. It seemed to him that he had received some momentous intelligence and that he needed to absorb it, but at the same time he was uncertain why any of this should concern him at all, let alone disturb him.

"Is something the matter, darling?" Lydia asked.

"No. Not at all."

"Well . . . are you going to open the champagne?"

"Yup."

All three women were looking at him now. They seemed to be waiting for some explanation as to what was all of a sudden filling him with this apparent reluctance to open the bottle. He was aware of something perilous in his own immobilized silence; that the longer it continued, the more he stood to lose. And yet for some time he was unable to move.

Annals of the
Honorary Secretary

It isn't known when Lucille Thomas first appeared among us. Who brought her, or at least told her where our circle met, remains equally mysterious. One or two members have claimed the distinction, but with little to offer yet in the way of evidence. Most of her casual remarks from the period before her first performance have passed into oblivion; those that survive have the overcherished luster of apocrypha.

The consensus is that she had been coming to our meetings for perhaps as long as a year before she made her debut. During that time she maintained an attitude of more or less silent watchfulness. I don't recall her asking anything during question times or taking the opportunity during our less formal discussions to advertise herself by saying something clever or controversial.

I myself had taken little notice of her until just a few days before her first performance, when certain familiar signs—a definite concentration of purpose visible in the outward manner; a sudden close interest in matters of procedure—suggested to me the imminent breaking of a silence.

At that time we were meeting at the Kurwens' house up near the North Circular. The large double drawing room was crowded with people standing in groups or sitting on the Kurwens' velour chairs and sofas. We had just listened to a talk, and there was the usual murmur of discussion. I was sitting between Brenda and Donald Kurwen, and I remember gesturing toward the back of the room, where Lucille, as yet unknown to us, sat on the window seat, and saying that I thought we would be hearing from her before long.

"Good, good," Brenda said. "Any idea who she is?"

"No."

Donald took his pipe from his mouth and smiled. "All the better."

There was nothing unusual in our not knowing the woman's name. Our doors have always been open to any individual who cares to join us. The perplexing and often tedious nature of our presentations tends to put off all but the kind of people whom we would welcome anyway. Occasionally a charlatan has tried to impose on us, usually in the hope of attracting the attention of one of our patrons. Most people, however, come in good faith, and we have never felt a need to regulate our membership with formalities of introduction or recommendation.

The Kurwens and I looked across the room at the young woman. She was sipping coffee with the cup and saucer held close to her lips as if she was nervous about spilling it on the carpet. Behind her slightly bulbous head the afternoon light showed her untidy brown hair to be thin and emphasized the irregularities of her long, bony face. Quite a few similar-looking young women and men have passed through our doors over the years (I was one myself), and there was nothing to suggest that this one would turn out to be any different from the general type— sober and serious, not gifted, but educated enough to make a useful contribution.

On a Saturday afternoon in October, I took the tube to Bounds Green station and walked from there to the Kurwens' house. It was a cold, damp day, and the long residential streets were lifeless except for the occasional colored flicker of a television screen in a front window. I remember a melancholy feeling from the dreariness of the walk, the gray sky, and the smell of new, wet asphalt.

There were perhaps twenty people in the Kurwens' drawing room, not a bad turnout for a rainy afternoon. Most of the older crowd were there: Ellen Crowcroft, Marc and Sabine Chenier, Janice Hall, the Kurwens of course. No doubt like me they had made the effort out of courtesy for a newcomer; it had been announced that the young woman, Lucille Thomas, was going to make her debut.

I sat in an armchair next to Ellen Crowcroft. She had put her hearing aid in for the occasion and was wearing face powder, grains of which were visible in the wrinkles around her chin. On the other side of me, in a row of wooden chairs, were several younger people who seemed to know one another. Ellen turned to me, her large, asthmatic chest heaving a little wheezily under her dress.

"New blood tonight," she whispered, and we shared the skeptical but ever-hopeful smile of a pair of old-timers.

The clock over the raised platform at the end of the room struck four. This was the official starting time, but as always we waited a few minutes for latecomers. A pale, wintry light came through the bay windows, lying with a hard gleam on the Kurwens' ornate coffee urn, beside which stood rows of green cups and saucers.

Trevor McWilliam, who was giving the first presentation, sat on a chair in the front row, shuffling through his papers. He was a self-effacing man who had been with us for several years. He wasn't gifted, but his theoretical work was usually interesting, even if it tended more to consolidate ground already covered than actually to take us forward in our investigations.

In the same row, separated by five or six empty chairs, sat Lucille. She didn't appear to have papers or any other equipment with her. I assumed this meant she was going to extemporize a talk, and I remember feeling anxious on her behalf.

Donald Kurwen strolled to the front of the room, puffing at his pipe.

"I think we might as well begin," he said.

Trevor spoke for an hour. As ever, his presentation was scholarly, a little meandering, with one or two pedantic jokes, which we laughed at dutifully. Some of our members, who were following his researches more closely than I was, jotted things down in notebooks as he read. I myself was content to sit and let my thoughts wander where they chose; at a certain point one comes to recognize the limitations of a person's mind, and in a general if not a literal way, one knows in advance what they are going to say on any given subject.

There was a short question and answer period. Donald Kurwen stepped up to the platform again, thanked Trevor, and gave a few words of welcome to the newcomer, Lucille Thomas, who was to follow him. Evidently Donald had no more idea what to expect than the rest of us, and after extending good wishes and appreciation on behalf of us all, he smiled at the young woman and led us in the round of applause with which we customarily welcome a debut.

The young woman climbed onto the platform and stood at the very front of it, ignoring both the chair and the lectern. It had grown quite dark in the room by now. The lamp on the platform was behind her, filling the irregular hollows of her cheeks and eyes with shadow.

There was a pronounced hush in the audience, as there always is when someone takes the stage for the first time. This is a moment of hope and excitement for us all. However much experience may have taught us to expect disappointment or at best qualified success, the mere impression of possibility, of promise not yet unfulfilled, tends to fill even the most jaded of us with a sense of impending revelation.

"I'm just going to stand here," Lucille said.

She stood at the front of the platform with her hands at her side, her jacket hanging shabbily over her thin-looking torso, her hair hanging in lank clusters. It dawned on us that her presentation was going to be practical, not theoretical, and at once the already quite keen attentiveness of the audience became even sharper. The proportion of people who are actually gifted (or believe they are) to those of us who are merely curious and enthusiastic is of course minuscule, and "practical" demonstrations are correspondingly rare. Not only that; most of them tend to fail, whether because of unreadiness, self-delusion, loss of nerve, or simply some delicate imbalance in the atmosphere.

In a very short time, however, it was apparent that this presentation was not going to join the list of failures. Quite how the terms of its success were to be judged was less certain (they are still being debated), but nobody can doubt that something extraordinary was happening, and within seconds I think we all realized we were in the presence of a virtuoso.

Words didn't enter into Lucille's presentation, and words probably will not convey the experience any better, say, than the bundles of triple zeros in an astronomy book convey the physical dimensions of space.

Ellen Crowcroft, most simply and perhaps most accurately, said that as she sat watching the girl, she had suddenly started to feel as if she were dying. Janice Hall said that it reminded her of a morning when she had woken from a blissful dream and had lain for several seconds bathed in its ebbing light until with an overwhelming feeling of desolation she was left with the stark memory that her husband had left her the week before and was not coming back. In general we all felt it to be an experience of unillusion rather than the reverse. Some felt little more than the kind of lowering of spirits that a good drink can easily remedy. One of the younger members reported feeling suicidal. A man whose name I don't know said that he had been reminded of the radiation therapy he had once been given for a tumor, a similar distressing sense of prematurely surrendering the integrity of one's living flesh to a force from the inorganic universe, the same feelings of acute, unnameable anguish and danger. Personally what I remember is this: First an abrupt transition from wondering what the young woman on the platform was going to do into a realization that I was being acted upon by a power outside my own control. Next, a feeling of being very quickly drained of energy: a sensation of heaviness in my limbs, of torpid fatigue in my eyes and head. Then, for about a minute, an almost dizzying sadness, as if some mysterious essence that made life tolerable were sluicing out of me. Finally I just felt numb and inert, incurious about myself, the girl onstage, and the people around me.

I left directly the demonstration was over. I had recovered from my numbness sufficiently to be extremely perturbed by what had happened, and I wanted to reflect on its implications in peace. I walked to the tube station along the same streets that earlier on had struck me as so oppressively dull and repetitive. This time, though, presumably as a physiological reaction to what I had just experienced, these houses, the lampposts, the pillar-boxes, clipped laurel hedges, creosoted palings, cherry trees, cars, pigeons, brackish dusk, bloated clouds, and disappearing sun impinged on me in a quite different light, a light of delicate and mysterious enchantment, as if my relation to them had been subtly shifted so as to reveal animating nuances of shade and depth that had previously been invisible to me. A sensation of calm happiness spread through me: warm, comforting, and expansive. I went home with the feeling of excitement that accompanies the realization, so rare as one gets older, that one has just been shown something absolutely new.

Lucille repeated the demonstration several times for us over the next few weeks. Word spread, and with every performance the Kurwens' double drawing room became more crowded. Each time the same annihilating pall fell over the hushed audience within a few seconds of the girl's taking the platform. The same palpable sensations of energy being depleted, of depression, listlessness, and apathy being uncovered like successive archaeological strata under a sharp and probing excavating tool, were reported in discussion afterward. Few of us were in any doubt that something of profound importance was being revealed. What was it, though? From the answers Lucille gave to our questions, it was apparent that she didn't understand her gift any more than we did. Certainly it didn't seem to give her any pleasure or pride. On the platform she merely stood still, stooped, slightly derelict-looking, staring at the floor with her hands hanging limply at her sides. Afterward she looked and sounded, if anything, even more despondent than she had before. She seemed to offer herself as the victim of an unknown sickness offers herself for examination to a group of physicians, not so much in the hope of being cured as of redeeming an otherwise pointless suffering from futility by giving it at least the potential usefulness of medical data.

———

One day—it must have been Lucille's fourth or fifth performance—Donald Kurwen announced that she was going to do something

different this time and wanted us to stand closely around her so
that we could see.

She sat on a chair at the edge of the platform. There must
have been more than fifty of us, the full complement of members,
including ones who had not been seen for several years. With some
difficulty we crowded into a circle on the floor in front of her and
the platform behind. A single recessed ceiling light was left on,
dropping a beam directly onto Lucille. One of her hands was
balled into a fist, and after we had all settled into positions where
we could see clearly, she put her arm out, propping it on a crossed
knee, and opened the fist.

In the palm of her hand was what looked at first like a shred
of whitish dust but on closer inspection turned out to be a little
downy feather, no more than an inch long, with a needle-thin
white spine out of which grew first a nimbus of fluff and then, for
about a third of an inch, neatly tapering white filaments clinging
to one another with their minute jellyish barbules to form a trian-
gular tip. Certainly it looked closely related to dust, and by that
branch of the family a cousin of absolute nothingness. But obviously the whole of creation stands between this latter pair, and
most of evolution between the former, and for all its frailty and in-
substantiality, the little feather's involvement with existence was
tight and intricate. I emphasize this because as it began to disappear under our eyes, melting away gradually but steadily from the
outer fringes, what we experienced was not the pleasing but almost insignificant difference between its being in the palm of Lucille's hand and its not being there that would have been produced
by a purely aesthetic perception of the disappearance, but a feeling
of something quite powerfully discomforting, both physically and,
for want of a better word, ethically, as if in standing around Lucille
we had come under the stress of some immense accelerative or cen-
trifugal force, and from the thickened continuum of space between

ourselves and the surrounding objects, something was being torn with a savage and stupendous violence.

Two or three more frail things passed into nothingness under Lucille's impassive gaze that winter: a dead bluebottle, a hairpin, a tiny sprig of evergreen leaves, these latter apparently involving more effort than she had expected; after beginning to fade at their outer edges, they started tremulously recovering their shape instead of disappearing, as if struggling to reassert themselves in defiance of whatever force Lucille was deploying against them. But after a few minutes they lost ground again and this time steadily faded away.

———

Spring arrived, and with it our New Year's party. Following the practices of civilizations better versed in the rites of renewal and reinvigoration than our own (one thinks of the Persian Tatars, the Mandaeans of Iraq), we designate spring equinox as the first day of our collective calendar and see it in each year with a party at the house of one of our patrons. While the taboos of our own civilization make an out-and-out orgy (the orthodox model for such festivities) problematic, we do all we can with food, drink, music, and dancing to induce in ourselves at least an approximation of the state of eudaemonia considered necessary to the sacred moment.

This year the party was to be held at the house of Helen Van Kemp, a wealthy and generous widow in St. John's Wood.

It was a cool, moist evening. I arrived at the gates of Mrs. Van Kemp's mansion at the same time as Janice Hall, and I remember Janice remarking that you could smell spring in the air. Torches lined the short garden path, burning with flickering yellow flames. A maid took our coats, and we stood a moment in front of the hallway mirror, checking our appearances. With the exception of a few theatrical types, our members tend not to be especially interested in sartorial matters, and to an outsider we would probably look a rather dowdy lot on most occasions. But for our New Year's party it was customary for everyone to dress up in whatever finery he or she possessed: for the men black tie or white tie, gold and crimson cummerbunds, war medals, silk cravats, and so on; for the women evening dresses, high heels, lipstick, and perfume. Janice, I recall, was wearing a green dress of a demure but close-fitting cut that suited her surprisingly well. She had had her hair done in a new style that made her look younger, and she wore a pearl necklace with matching earrings. I was reminded of how attractive she had always seemed to me when she had first joined us, long before her husband had left her and a kind of determined shabbiness set in, as if she were trying retroactively to rationalize his unexpected rejection of her. I told her she looked very elegant, and she thanked me, smiling at me in the mirror.

Helen Van Kemp came along a corridor to greet us in her usual effusively considerate manner. Like many very rich people, she worked hard at making one feel like an old and particularly dear friend from whom only the most extraordinary circumstances had kept her away in the interval that had passed. Her connection with our group dated from ten or twelve years ago, when Ellen Crowcroft—at that time more active than she is today—had put her in touch several times with her husband, Sir Clyde, who had been killed when his private jet crashed over the Isle of Man. I myself was present at the last of these occasions; it was spectacular and intensely moving. After twenty minutes or so the candlelit room had filled suddenly with an overpowering smell of jet fuel. We were all terrified the place was going to explode. An ecstatic-looking spasm seized Ellen. She tilted back her neck, and out of her radiantly smiling lips came the voice of a man, muffled a little as if by static, but perfectly intelligible, and with a kind of clipped, raffish tenderness that brought us all rapidly to tears. "Helen darling," it said, "I'm here. You're much missed. I can't stay. Think of me always." That's all. Ellen wouldn't accept payment herself and instead suggested Mrs. Van Kemp become a patron of our group, which she very willingly did. Since then she has funded the researches of a number of our more promising younger members and more than once taken her turn hosting our New Year's party.

This one was already in full swing. Janice and I followed Helen into the suite of grand rooms, some of them partially cleared for dancing. There was a wonderfully festive atmosphere. A jazz band corraled in potted palms was playing dance music. Many members had brought their families or other guests. Children in fancy dress were running around; white-gloved waiters were threading through garrulous clusters with trays of champagne. Buffet tables laden with salmon, cold sirloin, breads, salads, fruit tarts, and other desserts had been set out in the dining room. All the rooms had been garlanded with spring flowers. Boughs of lilac and forsythia were arranged around the windows; daffodils, lilies of the valley, and hyacinths stood in vases, filling the rooms with the fresh smell of spring.

The old gang were all there: Donald and Brenda Kurwen; the Cheniers with their shy twin daughters, both in pink and white frocks; Ellen Crowcroft, looking splendid in her white stole, leaning on a gnarled, silver-knobbed cane, her hearing aid gleaming in her ear more like some totemic ornament than a medical appliance. We stood together, chatting about the old days, and when we had eaten, we took to the floor for an hour or so of spirited dancing.

At midnight we went into an upstairs room where seats had been arranged around a raised platform. Our way of thanking our benefactors for their support was to present them with a demonstration by one or other of our more gifted members. Braidism, demonstrations of ectenic force, "community of sensation" experiments, and so on have always been popular on such occasions, and I suspect the atmosphere must resemble that of certain drawing rooms in the last century when celebrity performers did the rounds with their table tapping, invisible piano playing, and other tricks. Last year Ellen Crowcroft actually re-created an experiment that J. H. Petetin of the Lyon Medical Society had performed on Mme. de St. Paul in the 1890s, when someone in another room—in our case our hostess—put different foods in her mouth, while Ellen, with the pleasant smile that always appeared on her face as she settled into a trance, called out peppermint, mayonnaise, raspberry vinegar, anchovy, and so on with faultless accuracy.

Naturally we had chosen Lucille to represent us at this year's party. In doing so we were aware of departing from a tradition of festive, perhaps essentially trivial demonstration, but it was obviously out of the question for us to put forward anyone else. Besides, our benefactress had heard about Lucille and wanted to see her perform.

The revelation of any great gift always draws a wake of myth behind it as it settles into history. In Lucille's case, the mythologizing was in my view *concurrent* with the performance she proceeded to give. Confronted with things this strange and extreme, the mind tends, without realizing it, to translate what it beholds into terms more familiar to its own experience than those on which the phenomena themselves exist. In this case, since our perceptions were in themselves implicated in Lucille's performance, our sense of what actually happened must presumably be even further removed than usual from an "objective" memory. Furthermore, practically every one of us seems to have emerged with our own version of what happened, and while the gist of each version is the same, few of the details agree.

I myself, for example, remained unaware of most of the physical occurrences reported by other witnesses. I didn't see the flowers wilt or the lilac and forsythia blossoms wither and blacken on their boughs. I was unaware of the carpet of mold spreading over the half-consumed dishes of food in the dining room. The apparently overpowering smells of rotten meat and mildew that some people remembered so vividly didn't register with me at all. Nor did I observe the moths others saw massing in thick clusters on people's jackets and dresses. Although I would be the first to attribute these gaps in my testimony to the lack of a certain kind of receptiveness on my part, I remain convinced that what actually happened in that upstairs room was so far outside the experience of us all that each of us was obliged to re-create it simultaneously in a kind of emergency cascade of metaphors.

What I do remember, aside from the immediate pandemonium that erupted when Lucille took the platform and the sound of Mrs. Van Kemp crying out for her to stop whatever it was she had started, was this: a feeling of bitter revulsion, directed both inward and outward; a sense of having partially disintegrated, putrefied even, and of being surrounded by a pack of horrifying, corpselike beings. I remember looking at Donald Kurwen, one of my oldest and dearest friends, with a feeling of sudden, overwhelming disgust, as if he had begun shamelessly decomposing before my eyes. Janice Hall, in whom earlier on I had noticed what seemed a resurgence of her youthful attractiveness, looked to me suddenly pallid, bloated, and insubstantial, like some kind of fungal organism that would collapse in a puff of spores if you so much as touched it. Even her jewels seemed to have rotted, giving out not so much a gleam as a kind of phosphorescent glow. I recall vividly how the Chenier twins seemed to me for a moment like a pair of old crones dressed up in little pink and white frocks as though in a cadaverous mimicry of childhood. I pushed and clawed my way to the door along with everyone else, glimpsing Ellen Crowcroft turn and lunge back toward the darkness of the stage

with a panicky cry of "Lucille!" Outside, it was chilly and wet.
The torches had gone out. A few people lingered near the entrance, but most of us went quickly off into the night, making our
separate ways home.

As it happened, that presentation turned out to be the final act
of Lucille's career, at least as far as her participation in our own
circle was concerned. She never appeared at the Kurwens' house
again. None of us knew where she lived, and since it is not our pol-
icy to solicit meetings or initiate searches of any kind, we refrained from any attempt to find her. We all naturally have our
own surmises as to what became of her. Some of these are more
extravagant than others. Personally I tend to believe that her powers simply burned themselves out in that moment of frantic brilliance. And rather than linger among us, watching us grow steadily
disenchanted with her, she had the good sense to remove herself
altogether from our midst. To use an analogy from poetry, her gift
appeared to be lyric rather than epic, and like most lyric gifts, it
was short-lived. On the other hand, the critical exegesis has only
just begun.

CLEANNESS

It was his father's wedding day. Roland had flown into London the night before and slept at the hotel off Russell Square where he'd stayed during the last days of his mother's illness. The ceremony, at the parish church near his father's new house in Suffolk, was set for noon, reception at the house to follow. Roland woke late and found to his surprise that he had had an erotic dream. He tried to remember it, but the attempt itself scattered the last traces still lingering in his head.

He cleaned off its physical residue in the shower, then dressed carefully in front of the mirror; his father had always been a stickler for tradition, and the words "formal attire" had been printed on the invitation.

The rented outfit, which came complete with gray top hat, silk tie, starched shirt, and even a red carnation, fitted him well, and in spite of the absurd tails hanging halfway down his legs, Roland was pleased with what he saw in the mirror.

He set off across London in a green Citroën—also rented—and was soon on the motorway. It was a bright day, cool, with a few hooked scratch marks of cloud crisscrossing the blue. *Cirrus uncinus*, he said to himself. His father, a naturalist, had made him learn the names of clouds when he was a boy, and he still remembered them.

The old man was in his seventies now. His bride, Rosemary, wasn't much over thirty. In another man Roland might have been surprised at the gulf, but not in his father. Wiry and agile, with thick silver hair swept back from his forehead, sharp eyes still fiercely scrutinizing the world from his buzzardlike face, he had conceded little more than a kind of flinty hardening to the passage of time.

Roland had been introduced to Rosemary at a drinks party on his last visit. She was a biologist and had met his father on a scientific expedition to Tierra del Fuego. She was an intelligent-looking woman with an interesting face that made Roland think of a particular kind of craftsman's tool—a planishing hammer, was it?—in its smoothly molded planes and concavities, its look of having been evolved to perform some highly specific, complex function.

She had come toward him with an expression that had in it both shyness and something propitiatory. She seemed to want to convey to him her innocence of anything that might smack of an intent to interfere in his relations with his father, to assure him of her friendliness, and even in some way to ask his forgiveness for anything in the situation that he might find uncomfortable. They hadn't talked for long, but he had left feeling well disposed toward her.

He had seen her one more time on that visit. She'd come to London for the day and had rung him at his hotel to invite him for lunch. They ate at a Greek restaurant and afterward spent an hour wandering through the quiet streets around Hanover Square. Again the sensitivity, the propitiatory manner that soothed Roland and put him at his ease. He felt relaxed and, in response to her tactful but evidently sincere curiosity, talked to her quite volubly about his life: the well-paid banking job in Brussels that his father disapproved of (he disapproved of any profession that wasn't explicitly dedicated to the betterment of the human race), his unraveling marriage, his childhood.

His mother's unhappy existence had ended in a hospital not far from where they were walking, and as they approached the shabbier streets that had become so familiar to him from his daily visits, he began to feel all the harsh emotions of that period resurrect themselves inside him. Whether by chance or by some peculiar power of intuition, it was just then that Rosemary began to question him about his mother. Caught off his guard, which had been firmly up since her death, Roland had found himself delivering a long, fervent speech full of all the sorrow and exasperation that had lain pent up inside him for the past three years. Without criticizing his father, he tried to convey his irrational but nevertheless profound belief in a secret symbiosis between his father's vigor and his mother's steady decline. However much the old man harangued her for not pursuing a career, for not seeing a psychiatrist when she became depressed, for drinking too much, for smoking after she was diagnosed with cancer, there was some part of him (and for this Roland admitted he had no evidence beyond his own highly subjective instincts) that required absolutely that she remain on the downward slide, just as a healthy plant requires the steady disintegration of the organisms in the soil around it in order to thrive. And by whatever convoluted action of the psyche, his irreproachable concern for her welfare had precisely the opposite effect of what was apparently intended. It kept her in thrall to her own failure.

———

Within about twenty minutes of leaving the motorway, Roland realized he was lost. His father's map, which plunged from A to Z without regard for any of the opportunities for deviation that country roads offer in between, no longer corresponded to anything Roland could see.

He drove on, hoping to recognize a name on a signpost: without luck. Passing some houses, he considered stopping and asking for directions, but he felt awkward at the idea of going up a stranger's garden path in his wedding regalia, and before he could make up his mind to do it, the houses were behind him.

He realized that unless he found himself soon he would be late for the wedding, which would not go down well with the old man. By now, though, he was deep in the country. Fields of ripe barley lay on either side of him. There were a few barns here and there, but no houses. Small, unmarked roads appeared, each one necessitating a brief debate as to whether or not to explore it, so adding further to his consternation. Finally he came to the entrance of a driveway with the name of a farm on a sign.

The driveway twisted sharply down through a wood, then came out into a bare brown field with rows of scaly cabbage stumps. The unmistakable offal-like smell of pigs blew in through the car window, though another quarter of a mile passed before he came to the gate of the farm itself. He parked to the side of the gate. The elegant Gallic contours of the Citroën looked almost as out of place here as he himself did in his tails and red carnation. Through the gate was a run-down courtyard of pigsties with dozens of pigs—gray and hairy with pink patches—rooting and snuffling inside them. As Roland walked past, they crowded forward to the iron bars, making loud, harsh squeals and grunts. Their sties were several inches deep in slop. Huge mounds of refuse were piled in the corners.

Not just the pigs themselves but everything in the courtyard was covered in mud: buckets, bits of machinery, a small caravan occupied by chickens, even the chickens themselves. There was a forlorn oak tree with mud-covered leaves and a wheelbarrow so caked with mud it looked like a clay model of itself.

He picked his way with care to the entrance of the farmhouse and knocked. A woman wearing a short-sleeved dress and house slippers came to the door. She looked him up and down. He explained that he was on his way to a wedding and had got lost.

"Oh dear. I better get you a map. Come in."

She brought him into the kitchen, where she found a map and spread it on the table. She was about forty, large, with plump, pale arms. Her body in its thin cotton covering gave off a powdery odor—part perfume, part cigarette ash. Her eyes had a becalmed expression, almost dazed but every now and then settling on Roland with a soft attentiveness.

"Who is it getting married then?"

"My father."

"Ah. That's nice."

They found a route on the map. Thanking her for her help, Roland turned to leave. As he did, he saw a man standing in the doorway, holding a live white rabbit by the ears. Both the man and the rabbit were staring at him with expressions of amazement.

"He's lost his way," the woman explained. "He's going to his father's wedding."

The man said nothing. Roland edged out of the door past him, giving him a nod, which the man ignored. As Roland left, he heard a crunch and thud, and a moment later a white rabbit head, still wearing its look of amazement, sailed past him into one of the pigsties. The pigs converged on it in a cacophony of squeals. Roland noticed that a drop of blood from the severed head had splashed onto his polished black shoe. He turned back to the house, perturbed by the farmer's aggressiveness, but the man had gone inside.

The gate out to the drive where the Citroën was parked was

now blocked by a gigantic red tractor. Roland stopped, jarred by
the sight into what seemed to be a deep rift of memory. Where
had he seen such a tractor before? He had the sense of having recently seen a tractor exactly like this one, though since this was the
first time he had been outside a city in years, it was hard to imagine where it might have been. Even so, there was something familiar about it.

As he moved on toward it, he realized he wouldn't be able to
squeeze past it without dirtying his suit. He looked for another
way out. On either side of him was thick, wet-looking black mud.
A little way forward on his left, however, some planks had been
laid down in a line leading to a gap in a brick wall. He stepped
onto the planks, and walked gingerly along to investigate.

As he did, he thought again of the farmer's behavior. It occurred to him that the man might have been a jealous husband
wondering whether he had surprised his wife in the middle of a
clandestine meeting with her lover. Dressed as he was, he perhaps
had presented a certain archetypal, if also ludicrous, image that a
jealous temperament might have found irresistibly suspicious. Then
too, Roland surmised as he picked his way along the planks, perhaps he did have the face of an adulterer. A man's more significant
deeds might perhaps have a way of imprinting themselves on his
anatomy, if in a manner visible only to the unconscious eye of other
people. Had his marital infidelities left their signature on his flesh?
Had the farmer dimly perceived it? Was he at some level even correct in his appraisal of the situation, that Roland did have designs
on his wife? In a detached, clinical manner, Roland brought the
woman back into his mind, imagined being in bed with her, was
reassuringly unaroused, smiled to himself at the absurdity of it all,
then suddenly remembered where he had seen the tractor before.
It was what he had opened his eyes to on the nursery floor where

he and the children's Dutch nanny had first had sex. Unlike the
one here at the farm, it was a toy, pedal powered, but for an instant
it had seemed vast and strangely menacing, perhaps because his
three-year-old son was riding it.

By this point Roland had come to the gap in the wall at the
end of the planks and seen that the wall itself enclosed a pool full
of viscous greenish liquid that smelled like the contents of an
open septic tank. There was no means of getting to the grass beyond it, and he turned to walk back. It was at this moment that the
memory of the tractor had suddenly come to him, bringing with
it a great wave of anxiety that seemed to contain in it the whole
calamity of his marriage—the apparently inconsolable hurt he
had inflicted on his wife, the silentness that had fallen on their
young child, the bitter dismantling of the home—all of it surging
through him with a force that for a moment overwhelmed him.
He missed his footing on the plank. Groping at air to regain his
balance, he fell backward into the stinking pool.

A moment of absolute surrender followed. It was oddly luxu-
rious, and he was aware of extending it for as long as he could. Although the day was cool, the liquid was warm, and in this state of
surrender, what he felt seeping through his jacket and trousers
wasn't wholly unpleasant. He looked at the old farm buildings
around him, the crops beyond, the sky overhead; for a while he felt
almost blissful. It was only as he hoisted himself out of the pool,
rising from it like a swamp animal dripping slime, that he began
to feel the true foulness of his condition. There was no pain, not
even any great physical discomfort. But the sensation of a vile un-
cleanness both soaking into him and emanating out from him was
horrible. He trudged back through the mud (what need now for
the planked walkway?) toward the gate blocked by the squatting
tractor. There before him, he saw what he had managed to conceal

from himself before: just to the side of the main gate was another little one, which he could have passed through without any risk to his attire.

Tearing up clumps of dock (*Rumex crispus*), he did what he could to wipe himself clean. He lined the seat of the Citroën with a protective layer of stalks and leaves before sitting down on it. In this manner, reeking, oozing greenish muck, he resumed his journey.

———

He was more than an hour late by the time he reached his father's village. Coming to the church, he saw that the wedding service was already over, and he drove on to the house.

This was a large building of brick and cobblestones. A rounded glass conservatory, filled no doubt with his father's specimens, protruded gracefully from the ample front. A brass band was playing in a marquee with fluttering pennants at the back of the wide lawn, where a couple of hundred guests were being served champagne. Under the shaggy arms of a cedar, long trestle tables had been set up, garlanded with flowers.

Large family gatherings had always unnerved Roland. From an early age he had associated them with all the more troubling aspects of his mother's personality: the outrageous remarks— cruel, snobbish, or simply bizarre—that any group above a certain critical mass seemed guaranteed to elicit from her and then later the drunken outbursts of weeping, cursing, even violence that his father's response of dignified silence served only to fan to ever more destructive heights.

He thought of the strange way his mother's image had been transfigured in his own consciousness. Alive, she had been a perpetual source of pain and humiliation—hatred even. Dying, she had aroused a kind of morbid solicitousness in him, strong enough that he had taken two months off from his job to look after her as she moved from her flat to the assisted living facility, then to the hospital and from there to the crematorium. Dead, she had undergone a final change in his imagination, turning into something frail, blossomlike, but enduring, for which he bore unexpected tenderness and love. He heard her voice, sad and low, as if she were present again beside him. "It isn't me," she would say after each new attempt to make something of her life had been abandoned. The volunteer work, the college administration job, the gift shop . . . "It just isn't me . . ." A familiar dim helplessness washed through him. At moments he could glimpse something almost intentional behind his own calamities, an obscure, insidious solidarity . . . Abruptly, the dream he had woken from that morning in his hotel came back to him; the woman in it had been his mother. A sharp pang of dismay went through him. A wet dream about my own mother, he thought, almost wearily. What next?

Clammy, still smelling bad, with bits of straw and torn leaves sticking to the slime on his suit, he made his way toward the guests. Before he reached them, he caught sight of his father: as ever a little shorter than he remembered him, but his silver hair gleaming with that curious vitality that had the effect of making you briefly question whether you mightn't have got things the wrong way around, whether silver wasn't after all the color of youth, while brown, black, and blond were the colors hair turned in old age. Beside him stood Rosemary, slim and erect in her white outfit, her veil pinned back, flowers and seed pearls gleaming in the silk and lace of her dress.

Moving toward the crowd of guests, Roland had the impression of entering the locus of a single vast living organism. The old man had always had a gift for ceremony, display, for all those occasions requiring a particular complex of forces to be summoned into harmonious form. University chancellors regularly consulted him on their processionals and jubilees, as did the organizers of village fetes. What radiant entity had he brought forth here? As Roland approached, its epidermis seemed to shrink from him, as though fine hairs or antennae had detected something inimical to its own rustling brilliance.

His father saw him.

"Ah. There you are," he said, not unkindly. His manner too was less forbidding in reality than it was in Roland's imagination. But when he saw the state Roland was in, he stiffened.

"What in heaven's name—"

"I'm sorry—"

As Roland moved toward him, he stepped back, drawing Rosemary with him. She pulled her arm free, however, and looked at Roland with the same warmth in her eyes as he had seen when he first met her. For a moment it seemed she hadn't noticed his condition, but when he heard his father say, "Rosemary, be careful, he's filthy," and saw her continue on toward him, it occurred to him that she didn't care. Over his own swamp smell he caught the fragrance of lilies of the valley. She put her long, silk-furled arms about him and drew him close, her white dress surely staining in great oval blotches from his oozing suit. In her embrace he thought again of his dream: his mother's incontinent body whole, supple in his hands; her naked breasts warm and sweet in his mouth. Appalling! And yet as he stood there, he felt as if he were on the point of being cleansed of the confusions, the glutinous horrors of his day, and instead of letting Rosemary go, he drew her tighter to him, burying his head in her sweet-smelling shoulder, while dimly beyond her he could hear his father tutting and fussing. And a strange elation rose through him, as though the great miasma, which had hung upon his life so long it had come to seem a part of his own nature, might after all be about to lift.

THE WOMAN AT THE WINDOW

A young Englishman was walking down a street in the West Village. He had come to New York on an internship at the Manhattan branch of the auction house he worked for in London, and he was on his way to appraise a painting at the home of a private collector.

He was early for his appointment, and he moved along at a leisurely pace, gazing appreciatively into the boutiques lining the street. He liked New York. Superior versions of all the things he enjoyed most in life—clothes, cocktails, art books, restaurant meals—were available everywhere at half the price they cost in London, and wherever he went people seemed smitten by his unusually pure Englishness: his drawl, his unfailingly polite manner, his pallid good looks.

He had a girlfriend in London, who worked for a merchant bank. Every morning he spoke to her on the phone, and every night he sent her an e-mail, usually with some anecdote chosen to appeal to her sense of the ridiculous: the beggar he had given a handful of change to, only to be indignantly informed by the man that he didn't "accept no goddamn pennies"; the clambake he had gone to on the beach in East Hampton wearing shorts and a T-shirt, where it turned out all the other men were wearing linen suits and ties ... And this too, the gathering up of these little stories to share with his girlfriend, was a part of his enjoyment of the city.

He turned onto a quieter street of brick town houses with window boxes and small front gardens enclosed in iron railings. About halfway along he heard a voice shouting from above him: "Sir, sir, excuse me, sir ..."

He looked up. A woman was leaning out of a window on the top floor.

"Could you help me please? I broke the handle on my door, and I can't get out of my apartment ..."

He hesitated, unsure how to respond.

"I feel like such an idiot, but I don't know what to do ... I'm trapped in here!"

"Er ..."

"Do you think maybe you could open the door from the outside if I buzz you in?"

She spoke slowly in a high, rather plaintive voice. Her brown hair gleamed in the sun. She wore a pale turtleneck sweater.

"Well ... All right ..."

"Thank you! I'm in Four-A. There's no elevator. Sorry!"

The door buzzed, and he stepped into a dim hallway with cracked marble tiles and a row of brass mailboxes. As he climbed the wooden stairs, it occurred to him that he was being set up to be mugged. This was no doubt some old trick, well known to New Yorkers, but still good for a newcomer like himself. The woman had probably spotted him the moment he'd turned down the street—guessed he was English from his herringbone jacket perhaps or the old-fashioned brogues that he had polished that morning—and readied her accomplice, some thug who would be waiting for him behind her door with a knife or a gun ... He should go back outside immediately, he told himself, turn around and leave. But something—some perverse pride or gallantry—prevented him. He moved on up the stairs, not afraid, but with a feeling of melancholy resignation.

The door to 4A was a dull beige color, with an egg-shaped brass knob. He knocked. There was a movement at the peephole, then the woman's voice, softer now: "Hi . . ."

"What shall I do?"

"I guess try turning the handle."

He turned the handle, but it didn't seem to be connected to anything.

"I think the spindle may have come out."

"Oh. Well, try just pushing."

He gave the door a push.

"Nothing much seems to be happening."

"Push harder."

He pushed as hard as he could. Still the door didn't budge.

"I think maybe you need to take a run at it," the woman said.

He paused. The imagined mugging gave way in his mind to a more sinister scenario. He was going to be accused of breaking and entering, or whatever they called it here: caught on some hidden camera perhaps; blackmailed . . . Thoughts of some embarrassing drama involving the police and his supervisors at work went through him. And yet, with the same fatalistic resignation as before, he stepped back along the landing and ran full tilt at the door, hurling himself against it.

This time it burst open. He and the woman stood face-to-face. She looked about forty, her features lined but still youthful, a narrow charcoal skirt hanging below her close-fitting sweater. There appeared to be no one else in the apartment, a studio by the look of it, with bare brick walls, shelves full of magazines and plants, and a bed in the far corner half hidden by a screen. After a moment of startled silence the woman spoke. "Wow! You did it."

"So it would appear."

"That's wonderful! I don't know what I would have done. I was just—I was just trying to go out."

"Well, I'm glad to have helped."

She had been smiling, but now she began to look agitated, her eyes darting about the room as if seeking support from familiar objects. The situation, though evidently not dangerous, seemed to him freshly awkward. It struck him that having forced the door open, he had taken on the aspect of an intruder, even though the woman had asked him to do it. For a moment this made him actually feel like an intruder, stirring something unexpected inside him. And this in turn prompted the thought that he must leave immediately, so as not to appear to be trying to take advantage in some underhand way. He straightened his jacket. The woman glanced at him, smiling nervously. "I don't know how to thank you . . ."

"Oh, no need."

"Can I offer you a cup of coffee?"

"No, that's very kind of you."

"A drink?"

He laughed. "A little early for me."

"Oh. Well . . ."

"Goodbye then."

"Goodbye."

He went back down the stairs, smiling to himself. Already as he reached the street, he was composing in his mind the e-mail he would send his girlfriend that night. He would make the whole story into a little mock epic of suspense and misplaced apprehension, with the woman as a damsel in distress and himself as the naive but gallant knight, too chivalrous to ignore her plea for help. He would describe the gloomy hallway, the sense of being led into

a trap, the melancholy obligation to proceed nevertheless, the odd-
ness of breaking into a strange woman's flat . . . His little moment
of male regression he would omit, but he would try to describe the
woman herself.

Although what was there to be said about her after all? A New
York woman of a certain well-groomed type: more glamorous-
looking than her English counterpart, her face more concertedly
made up, her hair more showily coiffured, her manner at once
more direct and more remote, giving that odd effect of intimacy
and unknowability.

He pictured her again, facing him in the doorway with her
dazed, slightly frantic expression, the afternoon light refracting on
the surface of her hair. Her voice came back to him, high and a
little mournful: "I was just trying to go out . . ." Briefly a vague
disquiet entered him, as though there had been some complication
present in the picture that he had failed to grasp at the time. He
tried to pin it down, but it seemed to retreat from him as he pur-
sued it, and by the time he arrived at his destination on Washing-
ton Street he had decided he was mistaken. It was as he had
thought: the woman herself had been the least interesting aspect
of the whole situation.

———————

She went straight to the kitchenette and poured a vodka martini
into one of the cocktail glasses chilling on the shelf of the freezer.
Listening to his shoes stomp down the last flight of stairs, she
swept the chrysanthemum stems into the disposal unit and
stepped over to the window where she watched him come out
through the door and walk off down the block.

She sipped her drink, following his progress till he disappeared across Greenwich Street.

"Goddamn Englishman," she said.

The accent had thrown her, triggering some absurd reflex of guilty nervousness. That and how much younger he was than she'd thought.

The sun sank down behind the rooftop opposite, and the color drained out of the room; only the chrysanthemums still glowing yellow on the coffee table, as if they'd been dipped in some kind of luminous paint.

A mistake, those. The wrong note entirely. She must have realized that unconsciously. She'd picked them up on impulse coming back from the liquor store with the Stoli, then forgotten about them till he was already in the building, so that she had had to unwrap them and trim them and set them in their vase, all in the space it took him to climb the stairs, forgetting even then to throw out the stems, which meant that the entire time he was there she'd had to be thinking about whether he had noticed them and, if so, whether it was reasonable or paranoid to imagine he might infer from them that she was not in fact just going out but had just come in, in which case—

"Oh, who cares?" she said, tipping back the rest of the drink.

She stood, consulting her own restlessness. After a few minutes a smile rose onto her face. Was this what was going to happen? There were ways in which the world forced itself on you and you had no choice but to yield. But there were also ways of using your own weakness as a source of strength. In high school she and her best friend had discovered they could do anything the other dared them to do by telling themselves they would do it on the count of three, with eternal damnation as the penalty for chickening out. *One, two, three*, and without hesitation the highway at the end of the school road would be run across blindfolded; the cherry-bomb-rigged toy boat sent floating over the pond to explode amid the boys' fleet of miniature clippers; the mystery substance puffed, sniffed, swallowed . . . Cumulative observances had strengthened the rite over time until it came to possess an almost magical potency, with no need of the penalty clause to enforce it. She had continued to practice it in college and on into adult life, using it not just for feats of gratuitous recklessness but also for simple practical purposes. *One, two, three,* and she could dive into the icy lake her husband's family had owned in Maine. *One, two, three,* and she could make herself call up her brother at his law office in Atlanta and ask for a loan. It wasn't about willpower; it was about submission. That was the glory of it.

She strode over to the table and picked up the bowl of flowers, carried them into the kitchenette, and shoved them into the garbage. No more innovations. From the kitchenette she went over to the door and wedged the thick brass tongue all but a few millimeters in, using a paper clip the way she had figured out earlier that summer. And then, pushing the door till she heard the little click, she crossed the room to take up her position once again, beside the quartered glass of the casement window.

The sky was clear, just a small fleet of clouds patrolling the river, pink lit from beneath. Nobody of any interest on the street. She waited, thinking of the first time it had happened. She really had locked herself in, pulled the handle and its mechanism right out of the door and been unable to unfasten the catch. In a panic of claustrophobia she had called down to the first person she had seen passing, a man in a business suit, who turned out to be a shoe retailer on his way to check out a new storefront. It had been his idea, not hers, to take a run at the door after nothing else worked. When it burst open and they had found themselves face-to-face with each other, they had both felt it, the sense of something unexpected surging up, rising right through them. It was just a matter of surrendering to it. He had stood there with a confused look on his face, making no attempt either to leave or to come farther in. She had offered him coffee, then before he had been able to form an answer, had heard herself add, "A drink," at which he had smiled, very sweetly. She smiled back now, remembering.

A man appeared, coming east along the block from Greenwich Street. She studied him carefully as he approached. He was tall, lean, with long graying hair. Leather coat, jeans, scuffed cowboy boots. A little wolfish maybe, his chin unshaven by the look of it, but after Mr. Tweed Jacket that was maybe just what was needed . . . She gripped the handles on the window and slid it up. For a moment a feeling of vertigo passed through her, as if she had opened the window onto a bottomless void. *One, two, three*, she counted in silence. Then heard her own voice calling: "Sir, sir, excuse me, sir . . ."

A BOURGEOIS STORY

I read the letter with a feeling of unease, then put it in one of the partitioned receptacles on the desk in my study and packed my briefcase for work. From a mahogany periodicals rack I selected a publication to read on the tube, a digest of reports on lawsuits arising from shipping accidents around the globe.

Karen was in the room we call the breakfast room, feeding our baby daughter, Sophie.

Spring sunlight, whiteish, with a tint of green from the foliage of the communal garden, came through the window, and there was a sound of birds in the cherry tree in our own private garden. I noticed that the tree was coming into blossom.

I stepped into the room to say goodbye. Karen smiled at me calmly, continuing to feed Sophie.

"You never met Dimitri, did you?" I asked her.

She shook her head.

"He's an old friend of mine. He's sent me a letter."

"Oh." My wife moved the spoon from the jar of puree to the flowerlike mouth of our child, and back again. Lit from the window behind her, the planes of her high-cheekboned face appeared smooth and firm as stone. Her fair hair was already up; brushed back from her wide forehead and fastened in a tightly knotted bun. Her lips, full at the center, but neat and small like the tight coil of hair on her head, were closed, as they always were the moment she had finished speaking, a characteristic that gave an emphatic finality to her utterances.

"We were at school together," I said, "then at university, till he dropped out."

Karen tilted her face up again: serene, maternal, not especially interested.

"I haven't heard from him for years."

She said nothing, though she gave me a pleasant look, as if asking me to forgive her indifference. As a matter of fact I had always admired my wife's attitude to my past, which seemed to be that compared to the great fact of our having married each other, our previous lives were no more than unimportant sketches, first drafts full of clumsy experiment and fruitless detours.

I kissed her and Sophie goodbye, passing through to the living room that led into the front hall.

As if she now felt safe from the risk of a prolonged discussion, Karen called out: "That's nice of your friend to write. What does he say?"

"Not a lot. He wants to get together sometime."

"Will you?"

"Yes, I suppose so."

———

On the tube I found myself unable to concentrate on the law reports. I hadn't seen Dimitri for almost fifteen years, but I could still picture him with perfect clarity: dark, shiny eyes; the close-cropped reddish curls; barrel-chested frame, six inches shorter than mine . . . I'd always had to bend down in his company, and I liked to think of the slight stoop I had now as a record of our friendship, hardened in me like the crook of a plant bent too long toward the same source of light.

At university we'd lived in the same shared house, a Victorian building at the end of a run-down terrace. I hadn't thought of the place for years, and I remembered it now with a feeling of fondness. The big kitchen had been a hub of student social life, with its peculiar blend of hedonism and puritanical zealotry. Over the sound of reggae from the stereo Dimitri's voice would rise with its hornetlike buzz, explaining to someone exactly why Bakunin and Marx had despised each other, how guild socialism had developed out of syndicalism, what the differences were between Fourier's phalanstery and Robert Owen's New Lanark ... In the kind of riptide of oceanic brotherliness that can flood into the mind of a well-read eighteen-year-old, he had discovered radical politics: Marx and Kropotkin, then Kautsky, Plekhanov, Gramsci, G. D. H. Cole ... What luster those names had once had! That must have been '76 or '77, a time of grandiose political rhetoric and gesture in the whole country. For a time Dimitri had even started referring to British politics as the Great Duel, after Heine's phrase "The great duel of the destitute with the aristocracy of wealth ..." Gingerly following his lead, I had dipped my toe in the same waters. As the tube rattled toward Lincolns Inn, I found myself remembering the picket lines I had stood on alongside him, the torchlit marches of the Anti-Nazi League against the National Front, the time I had thrown a flour bomb at a speaker from the Monday Club ... I could still see the thickset face of the man, feigning dignified imperturbability as the paper bag burst open on his pinstriped suit.

By the end of our second year even the limited privilege of being able to study at university had become offensive to Dimitri's principles. To the dismay of his tutors, he dropped out and went to live in Leeds, where the little revolutionary party he'd joined had its headquarters, taking a job as a laborer with a demolition company.

I visited him there once, a spur-of-the-moment detour on a trip to Edinburgh with a girlfriend. We had phoned from the motorway and followed Dimitri's directions to a dilapidated housing estate on the outskirts of the city.

Our reception was subdued, to say the least. Dimitri showed little curiosity about my life, and when I asked him about his own, he answered laconically, staring out the window, as if our presence oppressed him and he were trying to draw strength from the sprawl of suburbs and derelict-looking factories spread out below.

That was the last time we had seen each other.

———

"I knew people like that at university. There was a whole gang of them who joined one of those parties and then just dropped out en masse. I thought they were complete idiots."

It was night. Karen and I were in the bedroom.

"Don't look at me. I'm covered in cream."

I turned away.

"Anyway, I'm surprised you'd want to start up a friendship again with a person who could treat you like that." Karen brought her lips tidily together.

"We're meeting for a drink. I wouldn't necessarily call that starting up the friendship again."

Karen shrugged and stood up to go into the bathroom. After a while I heard her step quietly down the corridor to Sophie's room.

I lay still while she was gone, thinking again of Dimitri. What could have prompted him to get in touch after all this time? The letter, which had been forwarded from my parents' home, said only that he was living back in London and that he would like to see me. There was no allusion in it to the fact that we hadn't seen each other for over a decade. In this omission I caught the loftiness, the note of slight condescension that had always been present in Dimitri's exchanges with me. And on the phone, when I had rung him up to arrange the meeting, he had sounded almost offhand, as if it were not himself but I who had broken the long silence between us. In his casual way he had suggested meeting in a pub up in Dalston, where he was living now, miles from where I lived or worked. I smiled to myself, remembering how tamely, willingly even, I had acquiesced.

Karen came back into the room and lay beside me, propped on her elbows. "I wasn't meaning to be rude about your friend."

"That's all right, I'm sure he deserves it."

"He's probably feeling rather lonely these days."

"Maybe."

"And foolish too."

I looked at her.

"I mean, with everything that's happened in the world. Like someone who put all their money on the wrong horse."

"Oh . . . No, I doubt whether he'd look at it like that . . ."

I got up and went to wash. From the bathroom I stepped down the corridor to look at Sophie. She lay peacefully asleep, her hands either side of her head like two little starfish. I stood for a moment, thinking of Karen's last remark. It was something I might easily have thought myself, but it disturbed me oddly to hear it voiced. Privately, I had observed the events in the countries beyond what had once been the Iron Curtain with mixed feelings; it had been strangely unsettling to find myself somehow vindicated in the caution, the capacity for endless equivocation, the final attachment to comfort and prosperity that had delivered me to where I was today. It had felt like getting away with a crime, on the grounds that the crime had suddenly been made legal. "It's all right," history had seemed to whisper complicitly in my ear, "you have nothing to be ashamed of . . ." The peculiar economy of my conscience had apparently come to depend on the supposition of a universe violently opposed to my own. Without it the thought of my own life was sometimes strangely suffocating.

Under the cotton blankets Sophie's little chest rose and fell just perceptibly: up, down, up, down, each motion regular and predictable, and yet still surprising to me. As always when I observed it, a feeling of urgent protectiveness came into me. It was more or less superfluous, however, considering the bars on the cot, the thick pile carpet beneath it, the baby alarm, the thermostat . . . Not knowing what to do with it, I went quietly from the room.

Karen had turned out the light in the bedroom. A glow from the pale sodium lamp in the communal garden threw shadows of the cherry tree's knuckled branches against the thin fabric of the curtains. I remembered when we had first come to look at the house. It must have been almost exactly two years ago because the tree was in full blossom. Karen was pregnant, and I had just made the move from community to shipping law that had dramatically raised our income. We had both laughed in disbelief at the sight of the tree from the bedroom window. The extraordinarily abundant clusters of blossoms bursting out from even the thinnest twigs had seemed comical, a massive overcalculation of nature, absurd and benign, like an enormous bank error in one's favor.

———

The pub was gloomy and quiet when I arrived. A pale gleam from the brass-bracketed lamps lay coldly over the cumbrous furnishings. Empty chairs and stools stood around like giant chess pieces.

A figure in the corner of a horseshoe booth gave a casual wave of his hand. "Paul, hello."

"Dimitri!"

For a moment I hadn't recognized him. His hair, longer now and unkempt, had lost its color, and his face was gaunt and sallow. He wore a lumpy gray coat open over a T-shirt, with a thin white scarf around his neck.

"Good to see you, Dimitri."

"You too. You're looking well."

I saw Dimitri take in my suit and overcoat with a faint sardonic glimmer.

On the table before him was a pint, a tumbler of whiskey, and a pouch of rolling tobacco. The drinks were fresh, but he accepted when I offered to get him another of each.

"Cheers," he said as I returned with three glasses.

"Cheers, Dimitri."

We drank rapidly. Dimitri was forthcoming at first, with none of the aloofness of his behavior in Leeds. He had been out of the country for much of the past decade, he said, working for a coffee-growing collective in Nicaragua until the fall of the Sandinistas, then in Cuba, where he had traveled with other members of his party, the WPSR, at the invitation of the government.

"That sounds impressive."

Dimitri shrugged, licking the gum on a cigarette paper.

"It was interesting, I suppose." He began to describe his travels, though as he spoke, I had the impression that the experience had become remote from him. His words sounded spent, somehow. He broke off.

"Actually I don't believe in the idea of individual countries anymore. Cuba or anywhere else."

"Oh?"

"As far as I can see, a nation is just an expression of the human inability to give a shit about the life or death of other humans beyond a fixed limit. Or put the other way round, it's a way of organizing and instituting people's apparently limitless desire to grind their heels in other people's faces."

I smiled. This sounded more like the old Dimitri.

"Do I detect a note of disenchantment?"

"With what?" A surprisingly hostile glare faced me.

"With . . . the human race, I suppose." Which was not quite what I had intended to say.

"Oh, for fuck's sake." Dimitri turned away, looking irritated.

He finished off his pint, then downed his whiskey and stood up to buy another round.

"And what about you?" he asked, returning with the drinks. "I ran into John Mackenzie." John had lived in our house. "He said you'd become a barrister. That must have been a slog . . ."

"It was hard work, yes."

"But they pay you well for it?"

I nodded, warily. "The money isn't bad."

"Mackenzie said you'd bought a house on one of those private squares in Holland Park."

"That's true. Not one of the very big houses . . ."

"He said you'd told him you took home over two hundred grand. In a bad year."

He grinned at me. I felt myself turn abruptly red.

"It's absurd, I know, but what can I say?"

"Good luck to you! That's what I say." Dimitri raised his glass, still grinning.

The pub began to fill up a little. As if jostled awake, a jukebox blinked and started pumping out music energetically. It crossed my mind that Dimitri had summoned me tonight because he needed money. I began to try to formulate a position. What could I lend him without upsetting Karen? A thousand pounds? Perhaps just a few hundred. Or perhaps better just to refuse altogether, politely but firmly, offer to help in some other way . . . He finished his drink. I pointed at the empty glasses.

"Get you another?"

"Thanks."

I bought drinks and returned.

"You still haven't told me what brought you to London."

Dimitri frowned. "What brought me to London?" He reached for his tobacco pouch. "Let's see now . . . Boredom. I think that's what it was. Yes, boredom, as far as I remember."

I looked at him, saying nothing.

"Not much going on in Leeds anymore. The WPSR fizzled out. They still exist, nominally, but we couldn't afford to run the building or the paper anymore."

"Oh dear—"

"Yes, isn't it a shame?" Dimitri's eyes glittered acerbically. "But there we are." He spit a shred of tobacco from his tongue and lit his cigarette, which flared, sour and pungent.

"And what do you do with yourself?" I asked. "Where are you living?"

"I live around the corner. Luxury pad. Floor. Ceiling. Doorknobs on the doors . . . As to what I do with myself . . . I, ah"—he dragged on his cigarette—"actually I'm editing a new magazine."

"Really?"

"Yes, I thought you'd find that interesting. Always makes things easier if our friends have a project or two on the go, otherwise why would they be our friends?"

I smiled uncomfortably.

"What sort of magazine?"

"Oh . . . International. Utopian. Socialism in the post-Soviet era. Communism after the death of communism . . . That sort of thing . . ."

"Good for you!"

"Funny how many people say exactly that when I tell them about it . . . as if I'd volunteered to rescue a child from a sewer . . ."

I felt that he was getting close to making his pitch for a loan, and I decided impulsively that I would surprise him with my generosity. No sooner would he ask than I would be writing out a check for whatever sum he named. I could already feel the impending satisfaction of doing this swelling pleasantly inside me.

"Does it have a name," I asked, "the magazine?"

"*Demos*. It's modeled on Jean Jaurès's paper, *L'humanité*. Do you know Jaurès? He was the leader of the French Communists in 1905. Called himself a Marxist-idealist, which was a deliberate contradiction in terms, given that Marx dismissed personal idealism as an irrelevance . . . As I point out in my first editorial—ha! That sounds impressive—Marx himself was in fact totally confused about this. On the one hand . . ."

Another wave of volubility took hold of Dimitri, rather unnerving this time. He spoke with a strange energy, reminiscent of his student days except that what had once been a straightforward zealous enthusiasm seemed to have turned into a kind of caustic inversion of itself . . . His eyes, red-rimmed now, narrowed harshly, as if he were trying to exorcise some vague disgust or at least exasperation, directed equally at me, his magazine, and himself.

"Jaurès described Marx's vision of the human race as a sleeping person floating down a river, just carried along with the flow. According to Jaurès, this may have been true enough once, but now the sleeper had been woken by the turbulence of history and was going to have to take responsibility for itself if it didn't want to sink. What I ask in my—in my editorial is whether Jaurès mistook his own personal energies, which were titanic, for a more definitive awakening of the species than was really the case. Because as far as I can see, we're already exhausted with our little spell of consciousness, and we just want to go back to sleep . . ."

He broke off with a grimace, standing up abruptly, as if his own words irritated him, and went to buy another round.

"Sure you won't have a whiskey?"

"Yes, thanks."

He returned from the bar a moment later. "I appear to be a couple of quid short."

I reached for my wallet with alacrity and gave him the money. When he came back with the drinks, he was once again taciturn. There was a prolonged and uneasy silence between us. I began to feel oddly apprehensive. I had the sensation of being out of my depth.

"You know, I didn't expect to see you again," I heard myself say, "after our last meeting."

Dimitri knitted his brow, apparently trying to remember. He looked quite blearily drunk.

"When I came to visit you in Leeds."

"Oh."

"I had the feeling you'd written me off as a lost cause."

He frowned again, turning away.

"It was a hell of a surprise to get your letter. Very nice, but pretty unexpected."

Suddenly he gazed straight at me. Here we go, I thought. I felt surreptitiously in my coat pocket; there was the little leather case containing my checkbook. Dimitri sat upright, breathing heavily through his nose, his broad chest heaving up and down under his coat. Slowly, with great deliberation, he laid one outspread hand and then the other on the table before him, and gripped the edge. For a moment he looked rather deranged, as if he were about to turn the table over. Then a sudden malevolent glitter appeared in his eyes.

"I read a book about ants recently," he said. "Made me think of you. There's a species called honeypot ants who feed off honeydew. You can't get honeydew, whatever the fuck that is, in the dry season, so they've had to invent a storage system. They have a whole class called repletes, compulsive eaters who've evolved this pouchy gullet that can be distended to gigantic proportions. In the wet season the workers stuff these repletes with honeydew till their abdomens swell up like balloons. They can't walk or do much of anything at all at this point, so what happens is the workers hoist them up and hang them upside down from the roof by their back claws like those bottles there"—he pointed at the upside-down bottles behind the bar—"and in the dry season just tap them for a snifter whenever they're thirsty, by stroking their heads. Easy as shoving a tumbler up at an optic."

He gave a chuckle.

"That's me, is it?" I said. "A replete?"

"Have to admit, it fits you pretty well, all things considered . . . No offense."

I smiled, trying to appear unperturbed. However, I could feel the insult traveling into me with a peculiar force and velocity, as if there were nothing inside me to resist it.

Having delivered it, Dimitri seemed to lose interest in further conversation. I couldn't quite believe he had summoned me here simply in order to insult me, and yet he appeared to have nothing else to add. Perhaps it was just the belligerence of the alcohol, I told myself, and in an effort not to end the evening on a sour note, I tried to change the subject.

"I didn't mention I'd become a father, did I?"

"No."

"Little girl, Sophie, seventeen months. Very lovely."

Dimitri looked at me vaguely. For a few minutes I kept up a conversation about fatherhood, more or less one-sided. Last orders had been called, and as I ground to a halt, Dimitri yawned and stood up, buttoning his coat.

"Time to head off."

We went outside. I turned to him, trying to prepare a suitable goodbye, one that would convey my disappointed fondness without stooping to rancor.

"You can have a copy of the magazine if you want," Dimitri said, before I could formulate my words.

"Oh . . . Thank you."

"Come up, I'm just over the road there."

I followed him across the road to his building. An uncarpeted wooden staircase led up from a narrow entrance that smelled of stale food. We climbed four flights and walked down a corridor to a bruised metal door. Inside was a room about the size of our breakfast room, with a mattress on the bare floorboards and a yellow-streaked basin over by the window.

Kicking off his shoes, Dimitri pointed to the far corner. "There, you can take one."

There was a pile of papers stapled in bunches of about thirty pages. I stepped over and saw the word "Demos" stenciled in large black letters on the top sheet.

"It's been out a couple of years. I'm trying to get another issue together. Maybe you'd like to write something."

I looked at him, assuming he was being sarcastic. He merely shrugged, and flopped down on the mattress.

I picked up a copy of the magazine, realizing that I hadn't fully believed the thing existed. It smelled inky, felt vaguely as if it were smudging my finger and thumb.

"How much do you charge for it?" I asked.

A muffled "Have it for the two quid I owe you" came from the prone figure.

I put the magazine in my briefcase.

"Well . . . good seeing you, Dimitri."

"Yeah, yeah. You fuck off now."

"Good night then."

———————

A light was on in the drawing room when I got home. I climbed the front steps and looked into the room through the gaps in the half-closed venetian blinds.

Karen was there with our friends Jane and Ed Maddox. Jane and Ed lived on the other side of the shared garden and often came over for after-dinner drinks. They both worked in the City.

Liqueur bottles and coffee cups were set out on the table. Liqueur coffees were one of Karen's specialties.

I stood in the cool air, looking in. This was my own drawing room, and these were my friends, but the prospect of joining them was more than I could face at that moment. Quietly, I turned my key in the door and crept inside, treading softly along the corridor and up the stairs.

I went into the bedroom and took off my coat. From downstairs I heard laughter. Seeing my briefcase on the floor, I remembered Dimitri's magazine. I sat on the bed and took it out, holding it to the pale light that came in from the garden lamp. It was a tatty, rudimentary production, a relic from the brief moment between the fall of communism and the rise of the laptop, put together with just a typewriter and a photocopier, by the look of it. There at the front was the editorial Dimitri had spoken of: "Idealism in History: Jean Jaurès and the Millennium." I ran my eye over the dense paragraphs, some of which had been pasted crookedly to the original copy, giving a lurching effect. Gray, broken lines from overcopying lay across the pages in a kind of visual static. I tried to read the article but gave up after a few sentences. The thing seemed unutterably wretched, slightly unwholesome too, a relic that hadn't quite finished decaying.

I put it aside, stood up, crossed over to the window. A peculiar, anxious restlessness moved in waves through my stomach and chest.

"Paul—"

My wife was standing in the doorway.

"Why didn't you come in and say hello?"

"I'm coming," I heard myself say. "I was just on my way down."

She gazed at me, her lips neatly together. After a moment she turned and went back downstairs. Shoaled clusters of petals on the cherry tree gleamed in the semidarkness outside, extraordinarily profuse. Beyond them, curving up from the mansard roofs of the houses opposite, bright stars dotted the blue-bronze sky, with innumerable fainter ones in between. For a moment it seemed to me there was something almost mocking in the abundance of these things. The insanely prolific blossoming tree; the thick, flowering borders of peonies, roses, columbines, and camellias in the communal garden beyond; the great yellow and brown plane trees with their branches already heavy under a mass of budding foliage, then overhead the teeming glimmer of an inexhaustibly profligate creation.

I went downstairs. Sounds of conviviality came from the drawing room. Karen was telling the Maddoxes that I had just been in Dalston.

"Catching up with a Trotskyite he hasn't seen since university," I heard her say, "if you can imagine."

As I opened the door, I thought of the ants Dimitri had described, the "repletes," and for a moment saw myself all swollen and distended, hanging upside down from the ceiling of my drawing room, waiting to be milked. Grotesque . . . And yet I realized it would be a long time before I would be able to rid myself of the image.

Ed and Jane grinned at me as I entered the room. I tried to make myself look cheerful as I said hello.

"Dalston?" Ed said.

I nodded.

"Good God! You'd better have a drink, old cock, then tell us all about it."

Oh, Death

The Peebles, father and son, came over to introduce themselves when we moved in, five years ago. Dean, the father, was slow to speak, awkward when he did. But Rick was talkative, his eyes roving inquisitively over us and our boxes of possessions. A fuzz of reddish stubble covered his neatly rounded head and pointed chin. His voice was soft, almost velvety, with a sprung quality, each word like a plucked banjo note. He told us he did a variety of odd jobs in landscaping and construction, tree work being what he enjoyed most, the more difficult the better. He would climb up in a harness and spiked boots to drop limbs from trees that stood too close to people's houses to fell conventionally, or he'd drive out in his pickup to haul storm-tangled, half-blown-over trees out of one another's branches, then cut them up for firewood. "Any jobs like that you need doing," he told us, "I'm your man."

Sometime after that visit my wife and I passed two small children climbing the steep slope of Vanderbeck Hollow. They were both in tears, and we stopped to see if we could help. Their mother had put them out of the car for fighting, they told us, and they were walking home.

Home, it turned out, was Rick's house. Rick had met their mother, Faye, a few weeks earlier, at a Harley-Davidson rally, and she'd moved in, bringing these two with her. Rick's father had already moved out. Faye herself we met when we dropped off the children. She didn't seem to care about our interference in her punishment. She was a thin black-haired woman with pitted skin, bright blue eyes, and a dab of hard crimson at the center of her upper lip. She didn't say much.

They had their first baby the next year, a girl. Rick used to tuck her into his hunting jacket while he worked in his front yard, fixing his trucks or sharpening his chain saw blades. He liked being a father—from the start he'd treated Faye's two elder children as his own—but it was soon apparent that his new responsibilities were a strain for him. After a day operating the stone crusher at the Andersonville quarry or cutting rebar with one of the construction crews in town, he'd come home, eat dinner, then turn on a set of floodlights he'd rigged up to the house and start cutting and splitting firewood to make extra money. He sold it for seventy dollars a cord, which was cheap even then. I often bought a cord or two for our woodstove. Once he asked how I made my living. "Gaming the system," I replied, intending to sound amusingly cryptic. "You must be good at it" was all he said, pointing to our new Subaru.

He bought a car for Faye, cutting wood later and later into the night to pay for it, renting a mechanical splitter from the hardware store and erecting huge log piles all around his house. A note of exasperation entered his talk; he seemed bewildered by the difficulty of making ends meet. Here he was, a young man in his prime, able to take care of his physical needs, to plow his own driveway, fix his own roof, hunt and butcher his own meat, and yet every day was a struggle. If it wasn't money, it was offenses to his pride, which was strung tight, like every other part of him. He was always recounting (reliving, it almost seemed) insults and slights he'd received from various bosses and other representatives of the official world, along with the defiant ripostes he'd made. When Faye got a job on the night shift at Hannaford and was kept past her clocking-out time, he called up the manager at the store. "I told that freakin' weasel to get off her back," he said to me with a satisfied grin. She was fired soon after.

To blow off steam, he would barrel up and down the hill in his truck, churning up clouds of dust from the gravel surface. Or he would carry a six-pack up to the woods above the road and sit drinking among the oaks and ashes along the ridge. I would often find a can of Molson by a rock up there in the bracken where he'd dumped it: his gleaming spoor. He was building a little cabin on the other side of the ridge, he told me once. It was state land there, but he figured no one would worry. What was it for? I asked him. He shrugged. "Just somewhere to go . . ."

Another time he told me he'd seen a lion up there.

"A mountain lion?"

"Yep. Catamount."

"I didn't know they lived around here." In fact I'd read that despite rumored sightings, there were no mountain lions in this area.

He gave me a glance, and I saw he'd registered my disbelief but also that he didn't hold it against me. "Yep. Came right up to the cabin. Sucker just stood there in the entranceway, big as a freakin' buffalo. I kept one of the paw prints he left in the dirt. Dug it out and let it dry. I'll show you someday . . ."

As a boy, when the Peebles property had marked the end of the road, he'd had the run of Vanderbeck Hollow, hunting deer and wild turkey, fishing for trout in the rock pools along the stream that wound down the deep crease between Spruce Clove and Donell Mountain. He wasn't exactly a model of ecological awareness, with his beer cans, his oil-leaking ATV that he used for dragging tree carcasses down to his truck, not to mention the roaring, fumy snowmobile he drove along the logging trails all winter, but he knew the woods up here with an intimacy that seemed its own kind of love. I walked with him up to one of the old quarries one spring morning and found myself at the receiving end of a detailed commentary on the local wildlife. To my uninformed eye, the trees and plants were more or less just an undifferentiated mass of brown and green matter, and the effect of his pointing and naming was like having a small galaxy switch itself on star by star around me. "Trout lily," he said, and a patch of yellow-centered flowers lit up under a boulder. "Goat's rue" . . . and a silvery-stemmed plant shone out from a clearing a few yards off. "Mountain laurel"—he went on, gesturing at some dark green shrubs— "blossoms real pretty in late spring. Won't be for another month or more yet. They call 'em laurel slicks when it grows in thickets like this. Sometimes heath balds. It's poisonous; even honey made from the flowers is supposed to be poisonous. See here, the burl?" He put his finger on a hard, knotlike growth. "Ol' timers used to make pipes out of 'em. My dad has one . . ."

In his lifetime he'd seen the road developed a mile and a half beyond the family property, the surrounding land sold off in twenty-acre lots, with capes and timber frames and swimming pools and chain-link fences and NO HUNTING signs going farther and farther up the hill every year, and he hated it all, though his hatred, characteristically, stopped short of the actual human beings responsible for these incursions. He was standing on the road with me one afternoon, complaining about the arrival of backhoes to dig the foundation for a new house on the property of Cora Chastine, the neighbor below him, when Cora herself rode out of her driveway on her chestnut mare. Seeing him, she began thanking him for a favor he'd done her the night before, pulling a din-

ner guest's car out of the ditch at one in the morning. Smiling gal-
lantly, he assured her it was no problem and that he hadn't minded
being woken at that hour. "Nice lady," he said in his purring voice
when she rode on, as if there were no important connection in his
mind between the person herself and her contribution to the destruction of his haunts.

He and Faye had a second child, another girl. A hurricane—
unusual in these parts—struck that year. Torrential rain had
fallen for several days before, loosening roots so that the trees came
crashing down like sixty-foot bowling pins when the wind hit,
turning the woods into scenes of carnage, the trees lying in their
sap and foliage and splintered limbs like victims of a massacre, the
vast holes left by their roots gaping like bomb craters. Within the
hurricane there were localized tornadoes, one of which plowed a
trail of devastation through our own woods. Rick offered to do the
cleanup for us, pointing out that there were some valuable trees
we could sell for timber. He proposed doing all the work himself
over the course of a year, to use a cousin's team of horses to drag
the timber out so as to avoid the erosion big machines caused, to
load it with a hand-winched pulley (a "come-along" was his quaint
name for this), to chop up all the crowns for firewood, and to haul
off the stumps to the town dump.

I prevaricated, knowing he had no insurance and sensing
possible problems if he should injure himself. A lawyer friend told
us on no account to let him do the work, and we hired a fully in-
sured professional logging crew instead. They brought in a skidder
the size of a tugboat, a bulldozer, two tractors, and a grappler with
a claw that could grab a trunk a yard thick and hoist it thirty feet
into the air. For several weeks these machines tore through our
woods; bulldozing rocks, branches, and stumps into huge unsightly
piles and ripping a raw red trail across stream beds and fern-filled
clearings to the landing stage by the road, where they loaded the

limbless trunks onto their double-length trailer to sell at the lumberyard. I ran into Rick several times on the road during the operation. He never reproached us for passing him over for the job; in fact offered good advice on how not to get cheated out of our share of the proceeds. But I felt uncomfortable seeing him walk by, as though I'd done him out of work that was his by rights.

He and Faye got married the following summer. We were invited to the celebratory pig roast. It was a big party: beat-up old pickup trucks lining the road halfway down the hill and twenty or thirty motorcycles parked in the driveway. We recognized a few neighbors; otherwise it was all Faye and Rick's biker friends in leather jackets and bandannas. At the center of the newly cleaned-up front yard a dance floor had been improvised out of bluestone slabs that Rick must have dragged from one of the old quarries up in the woods. Beside it a band was playing fast, reeling music: two fiddles, a guitar, a banjo, and a mandolin, the players belting out raucous harmonies as they flailed away at their instruments.

I liked this mountain music. I'd started listening to it a few years before and found I was susceptible to its mercurial moods and colors, more so than ever since we'd moved up here to mountains of our own, where it had come to seem conjured directly out of the bristly, unyielding landscape itself, the rapid successions of pain and sweetness, tension and release, frugality and spilling richness, rising straight out of these thickly wooded crags and gloomy gullies with their sun-shot clearings and glittering, wind-riffled creeks. I would listen to it in the car as I drove to work, an hour down the thruway. The lucrative drudgery of my job left me with a depleted sensation, as though I'd spent the days asleep or dead, but driving there and back, I would play my Clinch Mountain Boys CDs at full volume, and as their frenzied, propulsive energies surged into me, I would bray along at the top of my lungs with Ralph Stanley on "Bright Morning Star" or "Little Birdie" or

"Black Mountain Rag," harmonizing with unabashed tuneless-
ness, and a feeling of joy would arise in me as if a second self, full of
fiery, passionate vitality, were at the point of awakening inside me.

A van drove into the yard shortly after we arrived. In it was the
pig for the pig roast. As a wedding joke, their friends had arranged
to have the animal delivered alive instead of dead. Two of them
helped the butcher lead it from the van, roping its bucking, scarlet-
eyed head and shit-squirting rear end and dragging it over to Rick.
One of them handed him a gleaming knife.

"What's this?"

He stared down at the animal, writhing frantically in its ropes.

Faye had appeared, dressed in a denim skirt and red cowboy
boots. She looked on, smoking a cigarette with an air of neutral
but attentive interest.

"You gotta do the honors, buddy," one of the bikers said, "duty
of the groom."

There was loud laughter, a shout of "Go awn, cut his goddamn
throat."

"I'll cut your goddamn throat," Rick muttered. He went into
the house, and there was a brief, awkward hiatus. He came back
out with a shotgun. Faye turned away.

"Hey, you cain't do that, he has to bleed to death, don't he?" a
guest said, looking at the butcher, who gave a noncommittal shrug.

Ignoring them both, Rick loaded a cartridge into the gun and
fired it straight into the pig's head, splattering himself and several
others with blood and brains. This set off guffaws of laughter
among the bikers, and Rick himself cracked a smile. "I'll get the
come-along," he said. They hoisted the pig up with this device—
an archaic-looking assemblage of cords and gears and wooden pul-
leys—hanging it by its hind legs from a tree branch, and the
butcher slit it open, spilling its innards into a bucket. Then they
drove a spit through it and set it up over a halved oil drum grill,

and the band, which had fallen silent during this episode, struck up again, three high voices in a blasting triad calling out: "Weeeeill you miss me?" followed by the single morose rumble of their thick-bearded baritone: "miss me when I'm gawwwn . . ."

Rick came up to us with a bottle of applejack that he claimed to have brewed himself with fruit from his grandfather's old Prohibition orchard at the back of their lot. He insisted we take a swig from the bottle—it was pure liquid fire—then reeled away, grabbing Faye for a dance on the stone floor.

It was at this moment, watching him cavort around his bride with one hand on his hip and the other brandishing the bottle high in the air, while she stared out across the valley at the dusty emerald flank of Donell Mountain, that I registered, for the first time, the tinge of sadness in Faye's expression, underlying the more visible cold severity.

I was away much of the following year and aside from a few fleeting glimpses didn't see them again until the fall, when I ran into them at a neighbor's party. Arshin and Leanne, the hosts, were therapists, Buddhists, members of the local "healing community": Leanne shaven-headed like a Tibetan monk; Arshin gaunt and dark, a set of prayer beads forever clicking in his fingers. Their friends were mostly either acupuncturists or Chi Gong practitioners. Rick and Faye were standing in a corner, drinking beers with a tall man in a scuffed leather jacket and a pair of muddy work boots. The three of them looked out of place among these shoeless, tea-drinking wraiths. I went over to say hello. Rick introduced their friend as his "buddy" Schuyler. I noticed a string of numbers tattooed across the back of his neck, like a serial number. He gave a nod, then faded swiftly back into what appeared to be some immensely pleasurable private reverie. Purely to make conversation, I asked Rick if he was planning to sell firewood again this fall.

"Maybe."

"I'd like a cord if you are."

"Okay."

He didn't seem all that interested in talking. I moved away, wondering if I'd offended him by talking business at a social gathering. Schuyler and Faye left the party, but Rick stayed on, drinking steadily. At one point he started asking women to dance, even though it wasn't that kind of party. One or two of them did, just to humor him.

The next night, at two in the morning, he started firing off his gun. The same thing happened for the next several nights. I called to ask what was going on. He answered the phone with the words "Hello, you've reached the Vanderbeck Hollow Cathouse and Abortion Clinic," then hung up. A few days later I came home from the train station to find a pile of logs dumped over the lawn. It was true that I'd asked for wood, but normally we would discuss the price and the time of delivery before Rick brought it over, and he would help me stack it. I called him that evening. Without apologizing for dumping the wood, he said he wanted $120 for it.

"That's quite a bit more than you usually charge."

"That's the price."

I stacked the wood. It seemed less than a full cord, and I said so when I took the check down to Rick the next day. He was outside, talking with Faye by the stone oven he'd built in their front yard. He barely looked at me as I spoke.

"That was a full cord" was all he said, taking the check. "I measured it."

It was only when I spoke to Arshin a few days later, as I passed him on his porch clicking his beads, that I began to understand Rick's behavior, and it is only since I've spoken with a cousin of Rick's who works at the post office that I've begun to piece together the sequence of events in the month that followed.

Schuyler, their companion at Arshin's party, was not a friend
of Rick's at all, let alone his "buddy," but an old acquaintance of
Faye's. The exact nature of their relationship was not made apparent to any of us at this time; all that was known was that he had
turned up at Rick's house, having just come out of jail, where he'd
spent eighteen months for selling methamphetamine. Faye ran off
with him the day after that party, leaving the four kids behind.
She was gone for five nights. Those were the nights Rick fired off
his gun. She came back; they had a fight, a reconciliation; then she
took off again. The sequence repeated itself a third time, after
which Rick told her to stay out of the house for good. She could
take the children or leave them, he told her, but she had to go. At
this point Faye became violently angry, throwing furniture and
dishes at the walls till one of the older kids called the cops. Before
they arrived, Rick chamber-locked his gun and set it outside the
house. "That was so the cops would see there wasn't no gun violence in the house," his cousin told me. Faye had cooled down by
the time they showed up. Very calmly she told them that Rick had
threatened to kill her and the children and then himself. The police, obliged to take such threats seriously, carted Rick off to the
Andersonville Hospital psychiatric wing for a week's enforced ob-
servation. By the time he came out of the hospital, Faye had ob-
tained a protection order, barring him from coming within a mile
of the house.

The next few days are a mystery, obscured by conflicting reports and gaps in the record. What was known for sure was that
Rick spent them at the home of a relative, a woman named Esther,
whom he referred to as his "second mother," his first having disappeared when he was small. He was distraught, drinking heavily,
but also looking for work, intent on supporting his family even
though he wasn't allowed to see them. The Saturday after Thanks-
giving he took a job with a landscaper who'd been hired to do tree

work on a property in town. We first heard about the accident when Arshin called on Sunday to ask if we knew whether it was true that Rick had been killed the day before, hanged, up a tree. An hour later he called back to confirm the report. A heavy branch, roped to the ground to make it fall in a particular direction, had been caught by a gust and blown the wrong way, slashing the rope across Rick's neck and chest, asphyxiating him. He was seventy feet up in the air, and the fire department couldn't reach him with their cherry picker. They put out a call for a bucket ladder. A local contractor brought one and grappled him down. He was blue. The emergency helicopter on its way from Albany was sent back.

The funeral service was in town, at the Pinewood Memorial Home. It was already crowded when we arrived: young, old, suits, overalls, biker jackets, everyone in a state of raw grief. We signed the register and made our way inside. Loud, agitated whisperings rose and fell around us, anger glittering along with tears. Already there was a sense of different versions of Rick's last days forming and hardening, of details being exchanged and collected, variants disputed. The two older children sat on the front bench on one side of the chapel, fearful-looking as they had been when we first saw them, walking alone up the twilit slope of Vanderbeck Hollow. On the other side were Rick's relatives; his father sitting rigid, hands on his knees, broad back motionless.

Faye appeared from a side room with the two little girls and slid next to the older two, glancing briefly over her shoulder at the congregation, her face stricken, though whether with grief, guilt, or terror was hard to say. Even among her four children she seemed a solitary, unconnected figure.

A minister came in and told us to rise. He read from the Bible about walking through the Valley of the Shadow of Death, fearing no evil. We sang a hymn, and people went up to the front to speak.

High school anecdotes were recounted; fishing stories, the time Rick was chased out of his front yard by a bear . . . A tall silver-haired woman stood up. As she began speaking, I realized she was Esther, Rick's "second mother." She said she'd had a long conversation with Rick a few days before his death, when he was staying with her.

"In hindsight," she continued, "*unbelievably*, I see that I have to take this conversation as the expression of Rick's last wishes."

With a firm look around the crowded chapel, she announced that he'd said he still loved Faye. "He told me he still hoped to have another child with her, a son."

She paused a moment, then concluded: "Therefore, Faye, I honor you as his widow, and I love you."

An unexpected brightening sensation passed through me at these words. I, like everyone else no doubt, had arrived at the funeral believing Rick was up that tree in a state of impaired judgment, if not outright suicidal despair, and that this was a direct result of Faye's behavior. I still did believe this to be the case, but I was caught off my guard by the implicit plea for compassion in Esther's speech. In spirit, if not in any specific detail, it chimed with some dim sense I had of something inadequate or incomplete in the story I had been told of Faye's actions. I had concurred in the general verdict against her, but I must have had some faint scruple of doubt about the matter. At any rate I found myself thinking again of the expression I'd glimpsed on her face at the wedding, gazing off into the late-summer greenness of the hollow, and although I still had no more idea what it signified than I had at the time, I wondered if there was perhaps something more in the nature of a torment underlying her behavior than the purely banal selfishness and manipulation by which I had so far accounted for it.

The service ended. Whether by design or some unconscious collective assent, our departure from the chapel was conducted more formally than our arrival; a single, slow line formed, passing out by way of the casket. It was open, and there was no avoiding looking in. Ribboned envelopes were pinned to the white satin lining of the lid. "Dear Daddy," they read, in childish handwriting. I mounted the single step, bracing myself for the encounter. There he lay, eyes closed, beard trimmed, cheeks and lips not so subtly made up, chalky hands together holding a turkey feather. I stared hard, trying to recognize in this assemblage of features my neighbor of seven years. For a moment it seemed to me I could make out a trace of the old mischievous grin that floated over him even when his luck was down, and it struck me—God knows why—as the look of someone who knows that despite everything having gone wrong with his life, at some other level everything was all right.

That was November. Knowing what I know now—what we all know now—I go back to that ghost of a grin on Rick's face and find I must read into it a note of resignation as well as that appearance of contentment; submission to a state of affairs as implacably out of reach of human exertion as the shift of wind that took his life. And by the same token I go back to the look on Faye's face at their wedding and find in it, beyond the general sadness, the specific expression of a person observing that after all, nothing, not even the charm of one's own wedding day, is powerful enough to purge the past or stop its taint from spreading into the future. Whether this disposes of the "banal" in her subsequent actions, I am not sure, the situation being, in a sense, the precise essence of banality. Schuyler had been her foster brother from the time he was fifteen and she eleven. Arshin had the story from an acquaintance who used to work for the Andersonville Social Services. Over the course of several years, in a small house in the section of town known as the Depot Flats, he had—what?—"seduced" her? "Taken advantage" of her? "Raped" her? No word seems likely to fit the case, not in any useful way, which is to say any way that might account for the disparate, volatile cluster of wants, needs, aversions, and fears the experience appears to have bequeathed her: the apparent determination to put a distance, or at any rate the obstacle of another man, between herself and Schuyler, her equally apparent undiminished susceptibility to him, her cold manner, her strange power to make a man as warmly tender as Rick fall in love with her nevertheless.

She stayed in the house all December and January, though I barely glimpsed her. Arshin claimed Schuyler was living with her, sneaking up there at night and leaving first thing in the morning, but we saw no sign of him. In February we went on vacation. When we got back, there was a realtor's board up outside the house. Faye had left abruptly—for Iowa, we heard later, where she had relatives—and Rick's father had decided to sell the place. It sold quickly, to a couple from New York who wanted it for a weekend home.

A few days ago I met Cora Chastine coming down the road on her mare. We stopped to talk, and at some point I remarked how quiet Vanderbeck Hollow had become without Rick roaring up and down it in his truck. Cora looked blank for a moment, and I wondered if she was growing forgetful in her old age. But then, in that serene, melodious voice of hers, she said: "Do you know, I realized the other day, that Rick is the first person whose life I've observed in its entirety from birth to death, within my own lifetime? I was living here when he was born, and I'm still living here now that he's no longer alive. Isn't that remarkable?"

I nodded politely. She gave the reins a little flick and glided on.

I'd been planning to take just my usual late-afternoon walk to the top of the road and back, but something was making me restless; some faint sense of shame, no doubt, at having failed to protest that Rick's existence might be regarded as something other than merely the index of this genteel horsewoman's powers of survival, and instead of turning back I continued along the logging trail that leads from the end of the road up through the woods to the ridge.

It was years since I'd been up there. The trail was muddy and puddled from the late thaw, but the service blossoms were out, ragged stars, and the budding leaves on the maples and oaks made high domes through which the last of the daylight glowed in different shades of green. Reaching the top of the ridge, I followed the path down the far side, past the rusted swing gate with its STATE LAND sign and on down the uninhabited slope that faces north across Spruce Hollow.

The trees here were different: hemlocks and pines, with some kind of dark-leaved shrub growing between them, its leaf crown held up on thin, bare, twisting gray stems like strange goblets. It took me a moment to recognize this as mountain laurel—deer must have stripped it below shoulder level, causing this eerie appearance—and I was just trying to remember the things Rick had told me about this plant the time we walked up through the woods together when my eye was caught by a straight-edged patch of darkness off in the distance, and I realized, peering through the tangled undergrowth, that I was looking at a man-made structure.

Leaving the path, I made my way toward it, and saw that it was a hut built out of logs. It stood in a small clearing. The walls were about five feet high, the peeled logs neatly notched into each other at the corners. The roof had been draped with wire-bound bundles of brush. A door made of ax-hewn planks hung in the entrance. I pushed this; it swung open onto a twilit space in which, by whatever swift chain reaction of stimulus and remembrance, I became abruptly aware that I was standing in the cabin that Rick had built himself in order to have, as he had put it, "somewhere to go."

The top few inches of the rear wall had been left open under the eaves, giving a thin view of Spruce Clove. On the dirt floor below stood a seat carved out of a pine stump, with a plank shelf fitted at waist height into the wall beside it. An unopened can of Molson stood on this, and next to that what looked like an improvised clay ashtray.

I sat on the stump, struck by the thought that this would make a good refuge from the world if I too should ever feel the need for "somewhere to go." And then, as I was sizing up the shelf for possible use as a desk, I saw that what I'd thought was an ashtray was not in fact an ashtray at all. I picked it up; it was a piece of dried clay that had been hollowed by the imprint of an enormous, clawed paw.

A sudden apprehension traveled through me. Despite a strong impulse to swing around, I stopped myself; I dislike giving way to superstition. Even so, as I sat there gazing up at the granite outcrops of Spruce Clove, streaked in evening gold, I had an almost overpowering sense of being looked at myself; stared at in uncomprehending astonishment by some wild creature standing in the doorway.

CRANLEY MEADOWS

"What will I do? Keep looking, I suppose."

Lev Rosenberg remained stooped as he spoke to his wife, his eye pressed to the lens of the squat sixteen-inch telescope pointing through the small dome of the observatory.

It was a chilly, glittering October night. As Lev inched the telescope across the heavens, his wife could see faint showers of magnified starlight spark in the translucent part of his iris. The grounds of the college and the farmland beyond were visible through the open slot in the dome, familiar contours spectral in the bright moonlight. Frost was already glinting on the stiffened milkweed pods at the base of the observatory.

"Not that a fifty-four-year-old physicist who hasn't revised relativity is exactly a hot commodity on the market right now. As we seem to be discovering."

Bryony, Lev's wife, said nothing.

"Don't we?"

"I guess."

Last summer the college had fired eighteen professors, Lev among them. Only two so far had found jobs elsewhere. A few others had drifted off. Most of the dozen or so who remained owned homes in the area, with mortgages to pay, families to support. In a few months the severance money would run out. Then what? Were they going to have to sell their houses? Take their children out of college?

As a courtesy, Lev had been permitted to go on using the observatory. He came most nights; it seemed to be good for his morale. Tonight Saturn was rising in Pisces at an unusual angle to Earth, and Lev had brought Bryony with him to show her.

"You're not cold, are you?"

"I'm okay."

"Don't want the little fellows catching a chill. Can you catch a chill in the womb?"

"I don't know."

"Ah . . . There he is. There's Saturn. Come. Come have a look . . ."

Lev turned from the lens and smiled at his wife. His yellowish gray eyes were watering with the cold. Silver hairs shone in his black beard, which he had grown since being fired.

He stood back and made way for his wife at the eyepiece.

"That's a sight to put our little problems in perspective."

———

Lev had come to Shalehaven twelve years earlier from the Soviet Union. At the time of his arrival the college had been prosperous, hospitable to exiles like him. In those days it was prestigious to have a dissident on campus, and the college had shown its appreciation by building a small observatory to Lev's specifications. It was here that his relationship with Bryony had begun.

She was his student then, sixteen years his junior, tall—taller than Lev—with a reticent self-possession he had found beguiling. She'd stayed on at the college during the summer vacation of her senior year to write her thesis. As darkness fell on the warm evenings, she would make her way over to the observatory to record the positions of the star cluster she was studying. Lev would be there, writing or reading in his office downstairs. He would offer her a drink—not such a scandalous thing in those days—and they would talk, before going upstairs to look at the star cluster.

Toward the end of the summer their conversation had begun to take on a more personal tone. Lev told Bryony about his arrest for distributing censored pamphlets, describing the labor camp in Siberia where he'd built railbeds for a bauxite mine till he collapsed with a heart attack, aged thirty-seven. He told her about his years in internal exile in Tomsk, where he'd been caretaker of one of the old merchant buildings. He showed her a photo of the gray wooden building with its carved eaves and confided that he had been happier there than anywhere else in his life. "Until now. But you tell me about your life." She spoke about her parents, both doctors in Maine; her brother, a naval cadet; the year they had all spent at a reservation clinic in Alaska . . . "Not much to tell, really," but in the strangeness of Lev's new existence, the ordinariness of this calm young woman's life had had a powerful effect on him. They had first kissed up in the observatory, the smell of freshly carpentered lumber mingling with the faint soap scent of Bryony's skin and the sweetish tobacco fragrance from Lev's Tekel cigarettes, the air outside full of silvery spindrift from the milkweed pods that had ripened and begun to split. Even today Lev couldn't climb the braided metal steps to the dome without recalling the feelings of tumultuous affection those evenings had stirred in him.

———

Bryony peered into the eyepiece of the telescope. There, aswim in its powdery blackness, was the bright glow of Saturn, its rings edge on to Earth like a hatbrim seen at eye level.

"Pretty sensational, don't you think?"

"Yes . . ."

"Hm."

Lev sighed.

"It is sensational, Lev."

There was a silence. They could hear the low hum of the telescope's clock drive as it tracked the sky.

"Bloody Dieter," Lev muttered.

"Lev, it'll be all right. Something else will come up."

A couple of months ago Lev's old friend Dieter Kaufmann had called to say there was a position in his department down in Texas. Lev had applied formally and been chosen as one of three finalists for the job. A week ago he'd flown down for an interview. Today Dieter had called to tell him he hadn't gotten the job.

"Dieter tries to console me by telling me the job's not senior enough for someone of my standing anyway. What do you think about that?"

"I suppose that means they want someone younger."

"Precisely. Ha! At least I can rely on one person not to mince her words."

"They probably want a woman too, Lev. You know what it's like. Or someone from a minority group. Or both."

"Yes, yes. Well, I've always been in favor of that."

Bryony straightened up.

"You have another look, Lev. It's already moving out of view."

Lev caught a look in her eye as he changed places with her.

"What is it?"

"Nothing."

He gazed at her a moment. The supple skin over the delicate bones in her face seemed almost fluid in the moonlight, like glassily clear water over smooth rocks. She was still almost painfully dear to him.

"Are you worrying about me?"

"Well—"

"Don't. I've survived worse than this."

"Yes."

He kissed her lightly on the lips, then reapplied his eye to the lens.

"Anyway, I told Dieter the news."

"What news, Lev?"

"About the little fellows. What else?"

"I thought we weren't going to tell anybody yet."

"Well . . . I wanted to say something a little bit human. Otherwise the conversation was getting so formal . . ."

———

A few years ago they had tried to have a child, without success. A brief foray into reproductive therapy—Clomid, Pergonal, intrauterine insemination—had left them jarred and repulsed, and they had let the matter drop. But after the firings, Lev had suddenly decided he wanted to try again.

"I'm fifty-four," he'd said. "I'll be an old man soon. You'll go off with someone else, but at least if we have a kid together, you'll stay in touch."

"I'm not going off with anybody," Bryony had told him quietly.

But there was also the practical consideration that the college medical insurance would pay for some of the treatment, and they could stay on the plan for only a limited period.

This time, therefore, they had stuck it out. Bryony had gone back on the drugs. They made her ovulate prodigiously, and the surgeon had been able to cut out ten eggs. She submitted to this in a state of dreamy, half-fascinated passivity. The surgeon mixed the eggs with Lev's sperm and put three of them back inside Bryony. Two had fertilized. These were what Lev referred to as the "little fellows."

———

"Perhaps we should go back in the house," Lev said, still looking through the lens. "No sense in taking a risk."

"No . . . Let's stay here. I want to stay here."

"All right. Let's see what else I can find for you. I'm never sure how interested you are anymore . . ."

"I am interested, Lev—"

It was true, though; her own tender, almost shy interest in astronomy had become all but invisible, even to herself, in the glare of Lev's passion for the subject. Despite Lev's urgings to the contrary, she had long ago given up the idea of pursuing it professionally. In her vague way, she had come to think of Lev as being interested enough for the both of them.

She gazed out through the slot at the monochrome landscape. There was the carved white spire of the Shalehaven Unitarian church. A light was on in the house next to it. That would be Paula Kitson, who had also lost her job in the firings. The last time Bryony had run into her, Paula had told her a strange, rambling story. She had gone into town to buy groceries. When she came back, she had seen a bag on the table in her kitchen. The bag was exactly the same as the one she was carrying. Inside it were exactly the same groceries. "Can you believe it?" she'd said with a laugh. "I must have already been to the store and just totally zoned out."

Farther back, across the pale glint of Sawkill Creek, Bryony could make out the onion-domed silhouette of the old Hurley Mansion Carriage House. Sterling McCullough lived there.

"I saw Sterling yesterday," Bryony heard herself say. "Over in Cranley Meadows."

"Oh. How was he?"

"He looked bad."

"Poor man."

Sterling had taught political science for almost twenty years. He hadn't published much in that time, but with his distinguished white hair and bright blue eyes, his gift for vituperative oratory, he had inspired a devoted following among several generations of students. When the financial difficulties first appeared on the horizon, and cost-cutting measures were tentatively suggested, it was Sterling who had set the tone of fierce indignation with which the more combative among the professors, Lev included, had responded. And later, when the administration suddenly bared its claws and lashed out, abolishing tenure and firing a quarter of the faculty, it was Sterling who had organized the fired professors into an action group, the Shalehaven Eighteen. But it was Sterling too—after a euphoric summer of protests and press campaigns had come to nothing—who had taken the blow to his career most deeply to heart.

It was as though he had suddenly understood that along with his job at Shalehaven, the armature of his personality had been removed. In a kind of delayed collapse, like that of a building that has gone on standing for a while out of sheer habit of verticality after its beams have rotted, he had begun abruptly crumpling in upon himself. He started to look like an old man: his eyes grew dull; his voice thickened; his presence became gray and indefinite.

"You seem as if you have something you want to tell me. Am I right?"

"No . . . Nothing in particular."

She looked at him; the stooped bulk of his broad frame gave out an air of creaturely warmth. She felt an urge to touch him, or rather to be held by him.

"Cranley Meadows," Lev said. "What was Sterling doing all the way over there?"

"I don't know. He was sitting on a bench in the mall. He didn't seem to want to talk. I'm not even sure he recognized me when I said hello."

Bryony waited, willing Lev to question her further.

"There's Hamal," was all he said. "There's Mirach, Alamak . . . There's Schedir and Cassiopeia. Tycho Brahe's supernova. You know he built himself a golden nose after he had his own sliced off?"

"Yes, I remember."

"Sorry. I'm lecturing you. Hard habit to break . . . Here, you want to look at the moon? She's bright tonight."

"I'm okay, Lev. You look."

"You make it sound like there isn't enough moon to go around."

"I didn't mean that."

A clump of thin white birches caught her eye, gleaming in the dark woods like stripped wires.

"You remember Leibniz's famous question?" Lev asked.

"Remind me."

"'Why should there be being and substance? Why should there not be nothing?'"

"Oh yes."

"That's still the definitive question for me. I ask it every time I look through one of these and see all that mass of uninhabitable cinders and gases. Why should the universe go to all the trouble of existing? Back in Leningrad—"

The birches gleamed so brightly you could make out the little black eyebrow scars on their trunks. She thought of Lev's fondness for these trees. They reminded him of his happy days in Tomsk. He would run his hands over the taut, chalky bark of the bellying trunks with a sigh. On a walk a few weeks ago he had touched one of them and jumped back, pretending he could feel an infant kicking under the smooth skin. It had been on the morning of that day, in the doctor's office, that Bryony and Lev had first heard the twins' light, rapid heartbeats galloping toward them from the future.

"—Is it perhaps somehow necessary that there should be all this dead matter in order for one planet to flourish . . . I'm boring you?"

"No, go on."

"You used to claim you enjoyed hearing me free-associate about the universe."

"I meant it, Lev. And I still do."

"Hm."

He was silent a moment.

"What about you, Bryony?" he asked. "What were you doing at Cranley Meadows?"

There.

"Well . . ." she said.

But now that Lev had asked, a weight of dread seemed to paralyze her.

In the small room behind the blinds, with the Demerol ebbing throb by throb into her blood, everything had seemed to possess a transparent clarity of purpose. The image of Sterling McCullough's haggard face, its dim, unrecognizing glance as Bryony had greeted him, had added a layer of something resembling violence to Bryony's resolve. Thinking of him, thinking of them all, the Shalehaven Eighteen, Bryony had felt a curious sensation of remoteness. Their whole drama seemed utterly unconnected to her. They had been Lev's friends and therefore hers, but she had never felt, fundamentally, of their world. While they were still teaching, she had been unable to shake off the reflexive shyness of a student among professors. But now, in defeat, their ashen figures revolved in her mind like ghosts: exhausted and dimly appalling.

As the doctor entered, putting Bryony's feet in the stirrups and positioning the heavy suction apparatus, she had felt as if she were being carved free from some cold, gray, lavalike substance that had all but absorbed her into itself. It was as though some bright new creature were about to take flight from her prone body.

———

"Isn't that where they firebombed that place last year? The women's clinic?"

She nodded.

Lev looked at her kindly.

"Back in business, though, is it?"

"Yes."

Had she said the word or only mouthed it?

"Yes," she said again, louder.

Lev spoke quietly, after a pause. "Well, you know, I've always told you, anything you do, that's fine by me."

"I know that, Lev."

Again the urge to be held by him. She fought it again. It was harder this time, the urge bringing with it traces of old sweetnesses, insinuating sentiments, so that for a moment it was necessary to stand still and deliberately suppress the current of recollection— the first evenings up here with their delicate freight of tensions and broachings, Lev looming across her heart like the edge of a richly teeming shadow, the suede-soft milkweed pods just ripening, splitting open, setting adrift their glimmering strands . . .

She watched as he shifted the telescope, bringing the moon into his sights. A bright, snowy light filled the clear part of his eye. Slowly, as she observed the moonlight flickering on the foil-like back of his iris, she felt her composure return. She had the impression that she could make out the etched silver outlines of individual craters and lunar mountains glittering inside her husband's eyeball. It occurred to her that at one time she had known the names of most of them. Now she had forgotten them all.

Totty

After her divorce June agreed to let Alan keep the London flat and moved into the small house they owned in Sussex. It was a secluded place, an old farm laborer's cottage on the edge of a common, a mile outside the village of Three Bells Green. A century ago villagers used to gather firewood and graze animals on the common, but few people ever came there now, and it had reverted to brambles, with a thick wood in the middle, full of half-tame pheasants escaped from local pens.

The house itself had a small, neglected front garden with apple trees and overgrown rosebushes, and one of the things June had been looking forward to when she moved in was the prospect of restoring some order to this wilderness. She had also planned to take up the piano again, and to read all the books she had bought during the years of her marriage but never found time to open.

She had grown up in a cultured household where poetry and music were revered and a social gathering was an occasion for high-minded conversation. But in her own adult life things had taken a different turn. She had been beautiful as a young woman; full-figured with black hair and sharp-cornered eyes from which a deep blue light emanated. At twenty-two she'd had a child with a tennis coach who'd gone off after a few years to live in Australia. The child herself had joined him there later, when offered the choice at the age of thirteen. By then June was married to Alan, an executive at an oil exploration company.

The marriage, in retrospect, had been a series of increasingly sour amusements. First her husband had started having affairs, then she had. Most of their friends were having affairs. Politicians and the Royal Family were having affairs. Out of nowhere the word "totty" had started appearing on everyone's lips, and it was as if this word, which seemed to combine the bedroom with the nursery, had been the magic charm to release all London from its inhibitions, and the whole city had hurled itself into a wild, hilarious romp. For a while it really had been fun: it was nice being secretly admired and flirted with; keeping a furtive rendezvous at a Knightsbridge Hotel or a bed and breakfast out in the country; meeting a graduate student at a drinks party when Alan was abroad, and spending four days in a grotty bedsit with him; then exchanging that lover for another who insisted on sending her expensive jewelry that had to be vigilantly watched out for in the morning post, and then very carefully hidden from her extremely jealous, if simultaneously unfaithful, husband.

Being the more attractive of the two, she was better than him at infidelity. In an effort to keep up, he became incautious and indiscriminate, chasing almost every woman he met, thereby incurring a higher and higher ratio of rejection to success, with the cumulative humiliation requiring increasing quantities of alcohol to numb, which in turn made his behavior even more clumsy and crass. One night he'd stumbled home with red paint all over his suit. The next day one of June's closest friends, an artist, phoned June to say that she had flung it at him when he came barging into her studio and refused to leave. "I did it because I wanted to be sure you'd believe me when I told you what happened, darling," she'd said. "You know how peculiar we women can be when it comes to defending our menfolks' honor . . ." By now the whole rigmarole of her London life had begun to wear June down. Remembering the calm home of her childhood, she had felt disgusted, principally with herself. Her last act toward her husband—an affair with his elder brother—had been deliberately, vengefully cruel, and it had left her full of remorse.

So here she was, a woman of forty-two, grown a little fleshy; still capable of stalling a man's attention with a judicious spillage of blue light from her eyes, but increasingly choosing not to; and meanwhile living alone out in the rolling countryside of the Sussex Weald. Her divorce settlement would keep her going for a couple of years, after which she would have to look for a job.

She found it easy enough to keep busy. She had signed up as a volunteer for the local Meals on Wheels, and helped organize the village fete. She read, went for long walks, and sat at her old childhood piano, sometimes gingerly embarking on some half-remembered exercise, sometimes just staring at the battered old instrument, breathing in its smell of dust and wood and furniture polish, which was the fragrance of childhood itself. Already, after less than a year, she had begun to think of this as her "new life" and she was happy with it, more or less.

Across the road bordering the far side of the common, down a long driveway, was an Elizabethan manor that had recently been sold. In March the new owners appeared: a Harley Street surgeon with his family.

June met the wife first, a thin woman, drawn and pale, who appeared on the common one Sunday morning with two dachshunds waddling behind her. After establishing that June had until recently been a weekender like herself, the woman broached the subject uppermost in all newcomers' minds, namely the question of finding a reliable cleaning lady. June wrote down the number of her own, a Mrs. Dolfuss, who worked for a remarkably low hourly rate, came out on her bicycle in all weathers, and whose only annoying habit was occasionally to leave a religious tract on the kitchen table. Thrilled, Mrs. Crawford parted with the words "we must have you to dinner one weekend." An invitation duly arrived, for a Saturday in April.

It was a cool evening, with a smell of damp earth in the air. June walked across the common in a pleasantly vacant state of mind. She enjoyed meeting new people, but would have been just as happy to stay at home alone, and the knowledge of this was a source of calm assurance.

A new electronic security gate stood over the fresh gravel of the drive. The property had fallen into near ruin under its previous owners, but the Crawfords seemed to have done a thorough job restoring it. The roofs of the old outbuildings had been retiled, the garden wall repointed, the oasthouse adjoining the house itself converted into a garage from which a Range Rover and a small sports car glared imperiously across the courtyard.

Mrs. Crawford—Hazel—opened the front door, her two dogs scratching along on the parquet floor beside her. They leaped up at June, wagging their tails and licking her.

"Come in. Don't mind the dogs. They've just had their worm pills and they're after the salt on your hands. Not squeamish, are you?"

June smiled. "Not at all."

Inside, the house had been transformed from its previous ramshackle state into a comfortable bourgeois home with chintz-upholstered sofas and armchairs, and curtains of glazed pink cotton.

A man of about fifty, tall, very well dressed, and smoothly handsome, stood up as June entered the living room.

"Paul Crawford. Good to meet you. We're tremendously in your debt over this Mrs. Dolfuss woman of yours. She's I believe what's called a treasure, and fascinatingly rigid in her views."

"I did warn your wife . . ."

"No, we enjoy her immensely. Incidentally I'm curious to hear *your* views, on bloodsports, not religion."

"Oh?"

"I ask because my wife just now informed me that she neglected to ascertain them despite the fact that we plan to be dining shortly on a number of pigeons shot by my son and myself. May I offer you a drink?"

From the glint in his gray eye, she gathered that the man considered he was being interestingly droll. She smiled obligingly.

"I'll have a whiskey, please. And I'll gladly eat a pigeon shot by you or your son. I've shot a few myself in my time."

He laughed loudly at this, pouring her a scotch and handing it to her with a look of steely physical interest. The look was familiar to her from a thousand social gatherings: in the past it had seldom failed to ignite something in her, even if the man on whose face it appeared didn't especially attract her. As it happened, this particular man belonged to a type for whom she did have a certain weakness: confident, well made, and with an interest in women that consisted, in her experience, of a generalized contempt, in which a kind of aggrieved, violent desire was concealed like a stiletto. Acknowledging the attraction as she took the drink from him, she was nevertheless able to assure herself that she had no wish at all to pursue its implications. She looked away.

At dinner they were joined by the sons—there were in fact two of them, though only one appeared to be of any consequence in the father's eyes. This was the elder, Rob, who was there with his girlfriend. He was in his second year at Oxford, handsome like his father, with the same gray-eyed stare. He and his father had a routine that consisted of his scandalizing the older man with shafts of what were clearly intended to be shockingly bigoted opinions on various political matters, at each of which the father would yelp with joyous outrage, expound at great length his own more enlightened views on the subject, then go on to provoke yet another shaft from the boy.

The younger son, Martin, was seventeen; a shy, very tall boy with red hair and pale red eyelashes opening wide on large, child-like eyes. Though he said little, and stammered when he did, his pale face registered every shift in the atmosphere with a high degree of sensitivity. His father ignored him, dismissing his few contributions to the talk with an impatient frown. He could hardly even bring himself to accept the boy's agreeing with him against Rob, telling him on one occasion: "Do be quiet, Martin. You're developing an unfortunate combination of pomposity and shrillness." Turning to June with a smile he added: "I like to joke that our youngest is in grave danger of turning from a Martin into a Martinet!" June glanced at the boy: his face had flushed, but he said nothing, and she herself could think of nothing to say, though she would have liked to.

Meanwhile, the wife seemed utterly eclipsed in her husband's presence. He treated her with a detached solicitousness, apparently regarding her as an invalid, measuring out her wine in half glasses, and chastising her when she came in from the kitchen bearing a tray laden with heavy bowls: "Hazel, I've told you if you insist on carrying on like some Bulgarian weight-lifter, you are going to be a cripple within five years."

He turned to June: "My wife has arthritis in her spine. Martin, take the tray from your mother. Go on! Are you afraid it'll snap your wrist or something?"

Rob and his girlfriend left after dinner to go off to a party, and June made her exit a little later. Paul saw her to the door.

"I hope it hasn't bored you to dine with us *en famille*," he said, looking at her closely.

"Of course not. It's been lovely."

"Next time we'll try to rustle up a spare man. That'll make it more amusing for you, I dare say."

She smiled blandly, reiterating that she'd had a lovely evening.

"Where's your car?" he said, looking out at the forecourt.

"I walked. I always walk, when I can."

The man turned back into the house: "Martin!" he shouted. "Come and walk our guest home."

"Please don't make him," June said. "I'll be fine. I have a torch. There's even a moon . . ."

"Martin!" he called again, ignoring her.

Martin appeared, wearing a pair of running shoes with straggling, untied laces. Paul glanced at them: "God. Is there no fashion too crass for you?"

The boy bent down and tied the laces.

Outside it was chilly. Dew had fallen, glittering along the gravel driveway. The sloping fields with their black woods in every crevice were lit by the moon, rolling away to the dark horizon in pure brightness and shadow. Martin walked silently beside her, a tall, awkward-seeming presence. She felt for him in his tongue-tied shyness, and made an effort to converse despite her annoyance at having had him forced on her. She asked about his interests. He was monosyllabic at first, but gradually relaxed, and by the time they reached the end of the driveway he had become almost voluble; grateful, it appeared, to have found a sympathetic ear.

"Do you like Bruckner?" he asked suddenly as they crossed the road to the common.

"I like what I've read of her . . ."

"No, Bruckner, the composer."

"Oh. I'm not sure I——"

"He's my god. He's completely misunderstood. Everyone thinks of him as this soft, dreamy composer, but he's tough!"

Other enthusiasms followed: a mixture of composers, artists, and writers who had in common, according to Martin, a deceptive softness under which they were all "tough," or "rock-hard," or "hard as nails." And several of them were also declared to be his "god."

The footpath entered the wood that occupied the middle part of the common.

"This is a bluebell wood," June said.

"What's that?"

"You've never seen a bluebell wood? You're in for a surprise! Any day, I should think."

A clattering of wings exploded from a tree ahead of them, sending a black silhouette whirring into the sky.

"Perhaps we shouldn't talk. We're waking the pheasants."

They walked on in silence. It was very dark inside the wood, the ivy-wreathed trees snaking up against the moon, and June found herself glad of the boy's company after all. When they arrived at her house she invited him in for a nightcap.

"Just a very quick one," she said, immediately regretting the impulse. "I'm not good at staying up late." Then, worried that this might have sounded unfriendly, added: "I'll make you a hot toddy. I learned the recipe from a barman at the Closerie des Lilas. That's a bar in Paris."

He sat at her kitchen table while she put on the kettle and cut lemons. His eyes followed her, wide and innocent-looking in his oval face, which was mottled pink from the walk. He had fallen into his awkward silence again, and for a while she herself could think of nothing to say. She gave him the lemons to squeeze. Standing with her back to the range, she watched him in silence. His hands were very large, the long, angular fingers each with a glint of gold hair below the knuckle, the upper joints bending a little backward, as in the hands of angels in old paintings, as he pressed and twisted the lemon halves on the ridged glass cone of the squeezer.

He stayed perhaps fifteen minutes, most of the time just staring down into his steaming glass, but he looked happy to be there, and she found his presence relaxing. She had felt tired when they arrived but after he was gone she felt pleasantly alert and wakeful. Thinking, with a smile, of his "gods," she went over to her piano and began rummaging through her old music books. There was no individual book of Bruckner's, but in an ancient Schirmer's Library miscellany she found a piece by him called *Erinnerung*. A note translated this as "Reminiscence" and described it as a very early piece, written long before his better-known orchestral work. She began to sight-read it. It wasn't difficult at first: a simple, wandering melody for the right hand with slow minor chords for the left. But it grew harder as it progressed, and she lost her way. Even so, she had the feeling that if she could get properly back into practice, it was something she might be able to master. She went upstairs, leaving the piece open on the piano's music stand.

An hour or so later, after she had finished reading and was just falling asleep, there was a loud, single knock at the door. Some lingering after-impression of the boy had been in her thoughts as she was drifting off and it didn't occur to her to wonder whether it might be anyone but him. She went downstairs tying her dressing gown around her, and trying to think how to send him home immediately without hurting his feelings.

But it was the father.

She stepped back from the doorway, barefoot on the tile floor of the kitchen.

"Hello," he said. "May I come in?"

He entered the house, stooping under the lintel.

She looked at him warily.

"What are you doing here?"

"I've come to see you."

"Why?"

He said nothing.

"Are you drunk?"

"Possibly. In a sense."

He stood close to her, his tall, upright figure swaying just perceptibly. His cheeks, long and gaunt like tall shields slung from the high bones under his eyes, were flushed dark scarlet, his bluish-red lips set in a smile. She stepped back again, putting a hand on the kitchen table.

"Why are you here?"

"Because you are."

"What are you talking about?"

"I believe you know."

"This is utterly insane."

"I wouldn't necessarily disagree."

"You're mad. You've only just met me . . ."

"I don't anticipate a change of view."

"What about your wife?"

"Comatose. I administer her Dramamine myself. Admit you're not altogether surprised to see me."

"I *am* surprised. And not pleasantly."

"Really?" He put his hand over hers. She tried to snatch it away but he pressed harder, pinning it to the table.

"Let go."

His fingers encircled her hand, gripping it tight.

"Please let go of me, that hurts."

"Does it?" He squeezed tighter.

"Oh, for Christ's sake. What do you think you're doing?" With a violent twist of her body she wrenched herself free. "Get out of my house!"

He stood, eyeing her calmly.

"I see," he said.

"Get out!"

"Willingly. As I've always held, though I've not had occasion to say it to a member of your sex before now, or not in these circumstances, *ubi nihil vales, ibi nihil velis*. Incidentally—" he turned from the doorway to face her with a crooked smile, "—I'm correct, am I not, in thinking you're the woman who used to be married to Alan Houghton? Yes, I thought so. I've heard so much about you. I was at school with Alan. Nice chap in those days. Good night."

For some time after he left she was in a state of explosive agitation. She had met some swine in her time but none quite like this. She sat at the kitchen table, fuming. Almost worse than his presumption in coming here was the idea of his knowing about her past—her marriage and God knows what else. It brought back a bitter aftertaste of that time: the treadmill of jealousy and sour triumph, the constant vague rage. She wondered if he knew about her escapade with Alan's elder brother, and the thought that he probably did compelled her to revisit the mortifying memory of that little misadventure. In itself it had consisted of little more than a drunken night at the brother's flat in Belgravia while Alan was away on business, but the surrounding circumstance—the widely known fact of Alan's jealous rivalry with his more successful sibling, the disclosure of the event at a large family gathering where a nasty argument between the brothers about politics had led to Alan insinuating that the brother preferred men to women, only to have his own cuckoldry thrown in his face by way of evidence to the contrary, all this, combined with the incestuous flavor of the infidelity itself—had given the episode an almost mythically scandalous aura, and even to June herself it seemed to have occurred in a state of derangement, incomprehensible to her now, though the anguish it aroused in her whenever she thought of it remained as fresh and sharp as ever.

———

The next weekend was Easter. She was cleaning the house that Friday (there was no question of the pious Mrs. Dolfuss coming that week) when she heard a knock at the door.

It was Martin. In his hand he held a bunch of bluebells.

"I brought these for you."

"Oh . . ."

The dogs were behind him, gazing up at her with their look of nervous enthusiasm, pink tongues lolling.

"I picked them over there, in the wood. I've been waiting for them to come out."

"Well, that's . . . sweet of you."

"They're the same color as your eyes."

She gave a wan smile. The father's visit was still fresh in her mind and for a moment she wondered if he and his younger son were quite as different from each other as she'd thought.

"I'll find a vase for them," she said. "Wait there."

It seemed to her that an attitude of gracious but mildly severe composure was called for. She put the flowers in water and returned to the door.

"Listen, I'm touched, but you shouldn't have done that. For one thing you're not supposed to pick them—they're protected. And for another—"

The boy was looking at her, his expression solemnly attentive. A breeze flapped the tail of his untucked shirt.

"For another, I'm old enough—I mean put it this way, I have a daughter practically your age. Do you understand me?"

He looked blank, but he nodded.

"Well, so . . ."

Again he looked at her expectantly.

"So no more nonsense. All right?"

A crestfallen look appeared on his face, but he seemed to accept the rebuff, bunching his lips as he turned from her.

Back in the house she looked at the flowers. She'd had flowers sent to her enough times in her adult life for them to stop meaning very much to her. They were just things that had to be unwrapped and cooed over and arranged in a vase and then thrown out before they started smelling bad. But these seemed to take her back to an earlier time, when such offerings still had a power to move her.

She had done the right thing in sending the boy home, she supposed. And yet an unexpectedly strong emotion had come into her: an unnerving delight. Looking at these chalky blue flowers lolling on their stems over the glass bowl, she had a feeling of having just sacrificed the chance of some rare, harmless intimacy for the sake of an idea of propriety that meant absolutely nothing to her.

At once, as if that thought paradoxically freed her from a lingering resistance, she went over to the piano and began trying in earnest to learn the Bruckner piece, the "Reminiscence."

For the next three days she did little else. As she had thought, it was well within the range of what she had once been able to play, and the challenge of learning it seemed to her just what was needed to help her get back the old discipline and agility she'd had as a girl. Her concentration, grown weak in recent years, was remarkably focused once she started. It was no effort to sit at the piano for two or three hours at a time. Her hands ached, but she could feel them growing supple, her fingers recovering their memory of intervals and progressions. The music itself, even in the more complex passages, was a little bland, she thought, and she wondered whether the composer had really had anything much to "reminisce" about when he wrote it. But it had its effect on her nevertheless, filling her with a cleansing, clarifying sensation, and the more she played it, the more she liked being in its atmosphere.

Once, as she was playing, she saw Martin walking the dogs across the common. The family must have stayed down for the Easter holidays. He glanced several times at the house as he passed, and a feeling of gladness came into her: the looks seemed to confirm that she hadn't put him off entirely. It would have been easy enough to go out and say hello, but she stayed where she was, afraid of finding herself once again compelled to say something "responsible." She watched him instead, and it was almost as satisfying as talking to him, his loose jeans and untucked cotton shirt billowing down the length of his bony frame in the April breeze as he strode forward in his dreamy, gliding way along the path.

Thursday was her Meals on Wheels day. She picked up the meals in their heatproof cases at the Apetito center in the industrial park outside Mayborough, a few miles beyond Three Bells Green, and dropped them off with the clients on the estates nearby. She liked being with these elderly men and women, enjoyed seeing her own brightening effect on them as she set them up with the meals, often doing a bit of tidying for them while she was there. Some of the homes were squalid in the extreme, forgotten food rotting in odd places, overpowering smells of incontinence. But to her own surprise she had discovered that this made her want to stay around and help, rather than get out as quickly as she could. It occurred to her that she would have made a good district nurse, if such an office still existed, and at the back of her mind was a vague thought of training for that or some other sort of social work when the time came to get a job.

After she'd finished, she went to the town center to do some errands. She was coming out of the greengrocer's on High Street when she saw Hazel Crawford walking toward her with the dogs. She smiled, bracing herself for the encounter. But on seeing her the woman looked abruptly away and crossed to the other side of the street.

The snub, if that was what it was, didn't touch June in a personal way—Hazel Crawford was not someone whose good opinion mattered to her one way or another. But it was certainly peculiar, and its disquieting mystery fell over the cheerful mood she had been in for the past few days, not altogether dispelling it, but blurring it, like a half-opaque scrim.

The next day was Mrs. Dolfuss's day. She was an odd character, this Mrs. Dolfuss; honest to a fault (any loose change she found she would lay out conspicuously on the mantelpiece), but taciturn and singularly humorless, and she had always intimidated June. She spoke with the light burr and idiosyncratic grammar of the older locals, mixed strangely with a foreign accent, and June had a dim memory of having been told that she was a refugee, or had been brought over by refugees, though she had no idea from where, or how she had ended up in this rural corner. All June knew of her personal life was that it centered around a church somewhere in Mayborough, one where, judging from the pamphlets she left behind, a peculiarly bleak brand of Christianity was practiced. When June had informed her about her divorce, the woman had looked almost physically uncomfortable, as if the news placed her in a suddenly stressful relation to the house. Since then she had given an impression of being there on sufferance, coming strictly in observance of some regrettably binding agreement.

At the appointed hour that Friday she arrived on her bicycle, wearing a brown raincoat and a black plastic fisherman's hat. It was drizzling, but even allowing for that it seemed to June that there was something more concertedly forbidding than usual about the woman's appearance. Instead of letting herself in as she usually did, she knocked, remaining outside the door when June opened it.

"I've come to give my notice, Mrs. Houghton," she said, looking fiercely at her employer. "I did consider phoning but I come up meself in the end because I'm not ashamed to speak my mind. The fact of it is I can't be in conscience working here no more so if you'll kindly pay me to when I last come, I'll be on my way."

"What are you talking about?" June asked in a daze. "What are you saying?"

The woman's round, haggard face seemed to dilate in the gray air as though swelling on her own obscurely affronted rectitude. She shifted her weight on her feet: "What I'm saying, Mrs. Houghton, is I don't judge others because it's their business how they carry on, but where I work and who I work for is my business."

"What are you *saying*?"

"I'm saying there's some kinds of carryings-on I'll not be party to. So if you'll pay me what I'm owed in my wages I shan't be troubling you no more."

Abruptly June seemed to grasp what had happened.

"All right, I'll get your money," she said. She went inside for her purse, and thrust the money into Mrs. Dolfuss's hands. For a moment the woman looked nonplussed, hanging dripping in the doorway as though she expected June to defend herself, perhaps even beg her to reconsider, and it was a gratifying minor victory to be able to thwart her in that.

"What are you waiting for?" June asked.

Later, she regretted being quite so high-handed. It was obvious the woman had been manipulated, and equally obvious by whom. Vindictiveness was rare in June's experience, but she wasn't, after all, a complete stranger to it. She knew well the feeling of luxuriant, almost voluptuous destructiveness it released, over and above any justified punitive function it might serve. It seemed clear to her that something similar—some pure malicious pleasure—was discernible in Paul Crawford's behavior. No doubt there was a practical element too, at least from his point of view: preempt any attack she might launch on his standing as a family man, respected member of his profession, et cetera, by undermining her credibility among those who might matter. But she could feel something else too: some chill, gloating delight in the discovery of this power to harm her. Even when he had come to her door that night she'd sensed something much icier than simple lust going on. Certainly nothing as frolicsome as the word "totty" had seemed to be on his mind.

It rained all weekend and on into the next week. She stayed inside, brooding on what had happened. Who besides Mrs. Dolfuss had he maligned her to? What exactly had he said? It struck her that there was no reason for him to have restricted himself to the story about her and Alan's brother. He could be inventing all kinds of unpleasant rumors about her. It came to her suddenly that he had told his wife she'd made a pass at him as he was seeing her off from their house after that dinner. Yes: she could imagine it as clearly as if he were right there, speaking in that affected way of his: *Quite the little Miss Bedroom Eyes, that woman. She was all for dragging me home across the common with her on some pretext about the dark. I had to send Martin out with her just to keep her claws off me . . .* Was that why his wife had crossed the street? Meanwhile, what other things might he have spread about her? Nothing specific came to mind, but the sense of being spoken about, of remarks being made in the village shop, loaded questions asked in the bar of the White Hart, innuendos dropped into the conversation at the post office, was vivid and disturbing. The clear, invigorating air of her new life here in the country had been polluted, it seemed to her, a foulness spread into it.

What strange vacillations of feeling were being forced on her by her new neighbors! The boy's bluebells, the mother's snub, the piano piece, and now this. She spent the week shifting between these two moods. It was as though two mutually exclusive realities were being laid before her. One moment she would be playing the Bruckner, calm and alert, with a sense of being close to the source of some mysterious strength. And then a moment later she would find herself in the caustic atmosphere of the boy's father—hurt, enraged, and filled with her own, increasingly vivid, thoughts of revenge.

That Saturday afternoon, as she was about to leave the Sainsbury's car park in Mayborough, she saw a Range Rover with a familiar face at the wheel pull into a parking space. Keeping herself out of view, she watched Paul Crawford climb out and walk toward the Sainsbury's entrance. An idea came to her, a sudden image blooming in her mind, irresistible in its stark, obliterating splendor . . . She stood a moment, stunned at this resurgence of her old audacity, then smiled to herself, and took a pen and paper from her bag. She was about to start writing when she had a better thought, and went on into the supermarket instead.

It was crowded, but the man's tall figure in its tweed country coat was easy to spot: he was at the poultry section, appraising the respective merits of some pink young ducklings. He was handsome, there was no denying that. His cropped, silvering hair had a bristling look as if it might make the nerves in your flesh tingle. The line of his clean-shaven chin jutted forward.

You could say anything to people, she'd discovered in London, if you thought of yourself as an actor in a play, preferably some sparkling comedy. Impudence, malice, tenderness, brazen flirtation—anything was possible if you could summon that particular heightened, theatrical poise. Pausing a moment to armor herself, mentally, with spotlights and an audience, she moved in softly beside her neighbor.

"I was just going to put a note on your car," she said, not looking at him.

He took his time responding.

"Were you indeed."

"Yes. Shall I tell you what I was going to write?"

"I don't see that I can prevent it."

"Oh, I think you'll be pleased. I'll give you the exact words." She cleared her throat: "'I find I am unable to stop thinking about you after all. Let yourself in at midnight tonight. I'll be waiting for you upstairs.' There." She turned to face him. "No need to RSVP. Goodbye."

With a brief, candid glance into his eyes, which appeared once again to be appraising her with that air of detached, amused connoisseurship, she turned and walked unhurriedly out of the shop. On her way home she stopped off at the ironmonger's to pick up a small can of red paint.

It was late afternoon. By the time she got to the common the sun was melting orange through the treetops. Inside the house she poured herself a glass of wine. There were several hours to kill. She was aware of something volatile inside her: a strong, surging excitement, edged with faint dread. An uneasy urge to go over her plan repeatedly in her mind, assure herself of its invincible brilliance and logic, was making her restless. Small doubts began to assail her. Perhaps he wouldn't come. Well, that didn't matter. Perhaps, if he did come, he wouldn't leave, even after she'd thrown the paint at him. Not possible: he wasn't the type to risk getting into serious trouble. Well, then, the paint—wasn't that going to make a horrible mess of her cottage? Worth it, she assured herself. She looked out across the common. Occasionally at this hour you'd see a fox creeping under the tall tendrils of rosebay willow herb. Sometimes a barn owl glided by, heavy-bodied like a cargo plane.

Movement caught her eye—a figure deep in the woods, hidden and then unhidden by trees. No detail was discernible, not even enough to show whether it was a man or a woman, and yet she recognized immediately who it was. At once she found herself in a state of bright astonishment, in which several things appeared to be happening at once. Her "plan," in all its frail brilliance, seemed to collapse abruptly and evaporate like some flimsy illusion. But meanwhile another, still more incandescent invention rose up in its place. As it disclosed itself, she could feel the encroaching doubts vanishing abruptly from her mind. *This* was what was called for, she realized: an act of vengeance that would also be one of sweetly fantastical magnanimity . . . She wouldn't even have to spatter her walls with paint, she realized: the sight awaiting her antagonist as he opened her door was going to be all the red paint she could possibly need.

Opening wide the windows, she sat at the piano and began playing the "Reminiscence" piece.

It seemed easier than it ever had before. Passages that only a few days earlier had continued to elude her, unfolded with a fluency that made them sound, for the first time, purposeful. It was as if some final obstruction had been lifted, restoring abilities she hadn't felt since she'd moved from her parents' home, leaving her piano lessons and all other such childish things behind her. As her hands traveled over the keys, her mind raced forward, not so much planning events as foreseeing them, as if what awaited her was as clearly and unequivocally written as the notes on the staves before her, and would itself, in due time, become the indelible material of reminiscence.

He had recognized the piece, he would tell her as she opened the door. She would pour them each a glass of wine. Already she could feel his enigmatic aura spreading over her, not quite that of an adult, but not that of a child either. Not even quite of this world, it seemed to her. He was like a state of mind from long ago in her own life, miraculously recaptured and held out before her. They would sit on the sofa, talking. At a pause, she would bring up the subject of the bluebells. She'd regretted sending him away that afternoon, she would tell him. And taking his hand in hers, she would ask:

"Am I going to be given a reprieve?"

The gangly figure had emerged from the woods. Out into the darkening evening she sent the simple melodies. After a moment, she saw him look toward her house. Slowly, as if drawn against his own will, he began to move toward her, mesmerized, it appeared, by the phrases her fingers were conjuring from the instrument. She looked down as he came closer, but she could feel his steady approach, as if he were looming upward through her own consciousness. Then, as he came through the garden gate and stood at the opened window, she turned back up to face him, not troubling to feign surprise, merely smiling at him as he peered in at her, the edges of his light, loose clothes translucent against the low sun, his hair lit like a ring of red fire.

"Martin!" she said.

And for a moment she felt a sharp anguish welling up inside her, as if the convergence of wish with reality was, after all, an experience as close to pain as it was to pleasure.

Then, glancing at the clock, she stood up to let him in.

PETER KAHN'S THIRD WIFE

In a jeweler's boutique in Soho, the young sales assistant was modeling a necklace for a customer who had come in to buy a gift for his fiancée.

"Something out of the ordinary," he had said, and the assistant had shown him a cabinet with a necklace in it made of lemon- and rose-colored diamonds. The man had admired it but, after learning how much it cost, had laughed.

"Out of my league, I'm afraid."

"Let me show you some other things."

The assistant had led him to another cabinet. "These are more affordable. They're set with semiprecious stones."

The man had nodded and peered forward into the lit glass case.

"If you have any questions," the assistant had said, "I'll be happy to answer them."

For a while the man had looked in silence at the things inside the case.

"I'll tell you what," he had said abruptly, "let's have another look at that first necklace."

"The diamond?"

"Yes."

And so now she had taken the expensive necklace from its case and was modeling it for him while he sat in a chair opposite her, looking at how it lay on the flesh below her throat.

This was a part of her job, but in her seven months at the boutique she still hadn't grown used to it. It made her self-conscious to sit and be stared at by a man she didn't know, and it seemed to her that the men themselves were uncomfortable. Either they found it hard to look squarely at her in this moment, or else she would feel them peering too intently, as if they felt it their masculine duty to try to make a conquest of any woman who submitted herself so willingly to their gaze.

But this man was neither furtive nor brash. He was at ease in the artificial intimacy of the situation, intent in his scrutiny, but making no attempt to promote himself.

He was in his thirties, she guessed, dark and heavy-set. Brown hair curled on his head in thick clusters.

He nodded slowly. "All right," he said in a bemused tone, as though not so much deciding as discovering what he was going to do, "I'll take it."

A moment later he was signing his name, Peter Kahn, on the three credit card payments into which he had had to divide the transaction. Then he went out of the store, carrying the flat box with the necklace inside it in his coat pocket.

———

Over the next couple of years he reappeared in the boutique several more times to buy his wife anniversary and birthday gifts. The assistant, whose name was Clare Keillor, would model the pieces he was interested in, and each time she would experience the same calm under his gaze. It was as though for a moment she had been taken into a realm glazed off from the everyday world, where a form of exchange that was inexpressible in everyday human terms was permitted to occur between strangers.

She had no idea whether Kahn himself experienced anything resembling this, or whether he even remembered her from one visit to the next, but she found herself revolving the memory of the encounters in her imagination after they had passed, and when several months went by without Kahn coming back into the store, she would begin to wonder if she was ever going to experience their peculiar, almost impersonally soothing effects again.

On one occasion his cell phone rang while she was modeling a pair of earrings for him. He excused himself, saying that this was an important call, and she waited while he spoke. From what she heard him say, it became clear that he was in business as an importer of wines and that he was trying to persuade a partner to bid on a consignment of rare French bottles that were coming up for auction. Evidently he was encountering resistance, and his tone became increasingly heated.

"Taste it!" he said. He proceeded to describe the wine in the most extravagant terms, which in turn appeared to prompt even more resistance. "Well then, let's find customers who do give a damn!" he shouted. Then he snapped shut the phone.

Apologizing for the interruption, he tried to concentrate again on the earrings, but his mind was clearly on the altercation he had just had. The strong feelings it had aroused were still milling behind his eyes, and for a moment as he looked back at Clare, he appeared to forget why he was looking at her at all. He was just staring at her as though knowing there was some important reason why he was doing this, but not clear what it was. Then, as she looked back into his eyes, he seemed to stop struggling to remember and simply accept that this was what he was doing. And now for the first time she did have the impression that he was seeing her as she saw him, that he too was in that lucid atmosphere and was encountering her there with the same feeling of ease as she herself felt. Then the moment passed, and they were each back in the everyday reality of their own lives.

He decided against the earrings and left without looking at anything else.

———

Two more years passed. Then, on a hot morning in July, Kahn appeared once again in the store.

He stood in the entrance for a moment, adjusting from the boil and glare of the street to the store's air-conditioned dimness. He looked less youthful, fleshier and redder in the cheeks, but still handsome and with a more developed air of consequence about him.

"I'm looking for a wedding gift," he said, "for my fiancée. Something a little . . . out of the ordinary."

Clare looked at him for a moment before answering. He gave no sign of recognizing her, and despite knowing there was no reason why he should, she felt dismayed. A few minutes later, however, as she was modeling some new pieces for him, there was a startled motion in his eyes.

"Still here!"

"Yes."

"I didn't recognize you. I apologize." He gave an embarrassed grin. "What you must think of me, already on to my second wife!"

"Oh, I wasn't—"

"Well, it happens." He laughed, recovering his self-possession. "Anyway, we're very much in love. What can I tell you?"

"That's good. Congratulations."

He bought a set of earrings and an expensive emerald bracelet; money was apparently no longer a great concern.

"At least we can say I'm faithful when it comes to where I buy my wives their jewelry!" he said in a parting attempt at jollity. Clare gave him a polite salesgirl's smile. His phrase "We're very much in love" had grated on her, and as he left the store, she decided it must have been the formula he had used in breaking the news to the wife he had cast off, "We're very much in love . . ." as though he and his new girlfriend just couldn't help themselves. Clare pictured the wife—a blur of disembodied pain—and the girlfriend: younger, fresher, prettier. It struck her that Kahn hadn't recognized her because she too had started to age.

———

There was that realm, the glassed-in sphere in which these encounters occurred, and then there was the real world, and Clare lived her life in this world also. She married a man named Neil Gehrig, an airline industry analyst, twelve years older than herself.

At a dinner one evening, someone praised the wine, and the host said, "Yes, it's a Kahn."

Looking at the bottle, Clare saw his name on the sticker at the neck, "Imported by Peter Kahn," and an unexpectedly sharp emotion went through her. Three or four years had passed since their last encounter, and she was caught off guard by the force of her own feelings.

"He set up a company to bring over wines from the last small producers in France and Italy," the host was saying. "We grab everything we can afford off his list."

"I know him," Clare heard herself say.

"You do?"

"He used to come into the store."

"Really? What was he like?"

She shrugged, aware of her husband looking at her across the table, and regretting that she had spoken. "He seemed a nice enough guy . . ."

"Did he talk to you about wine?" the host asked.

The husband broke in. "Why would he talk to her about wine? It's a jewelry store."

"He's obsessed with it," the host answered. "We get this newsletter he writes. The guy's on a mission. He wants to save the wine world from globalization."

"How incredibly original," the husband said, leaning back in his chair.

"One time he took a call on his cell phone," Clare went on impetuously. "I heard him describe this wine he wanted to buy as like having the Rose Window at Chartres dissolving on your tongue."

"My God, a poet too!"

Clare smiled at her husband. Neil's jealousy had surfaced soon after their marriage and now lived with them like a third person whose volatile behavior had to be carefully negotiated. Once, after a dinner like this, he had hit her on the mouth with the back of his hand after accusing her of flirting with another guest.

That November Kahn appeared once again in the boutique. He wore a soft-looking felt hat and an alpaca scarf. His eyes had a melancholy cast. There was a woman with him. The second wife, Clare supposed.

He gave a half-surprised smile of recognition as he saw Clare. Still here? The look seemed to ask.

"We're, ah, we're looking for an engagement ring," he said.

It took a moment for the implication of this to sink in. Doing her best to conceal her surprise, Clare pulled a tray of rings from a cabinet.

The woman removed a pair of kidskin gloves. Her face was smooth and symmetrical. Its features seemed exclusively occupied in compelling the word "beauty" to form itself in the mind of whoever beheld them.

She glanced briefly at the rings. "I don't think so, darling."

Kahn turned to Clare with a shrug. "Sorry."

"Oh, no problem."

He gave her a smile.

"Shall we see some other things?" he asked the woman.

"I suppose, since we're here."

A necklace of rubies and small gold lozenges seemed to interest her.

"Why don't you try it on?" Kahn said. But instead of handing the necklace to his fiancée, he handed it to Clare. The woman gave a breathy laugh, and Kahn, realizing his blunder, put his hand on hers.

"Sorry. I'm used to coming here alone."

"Apparently."

"So you try it on," Kahn said to her.

Ignoring him, the woman turned to Clare.

"What's your name?" she asked.

"Clare."

"Put on the necklace, Clare," she said.

Clare put on the necklace. She was aware of Kahn's glance upon her, but she was careful to look only at the woman. After giving the necklace a cursory appraisal, the woman turned to regard Kahn. As the three sat watching one another, Clare felt as though her relation to Kahn had developed into something newly strange. Everything seemed suddenly its own opposite: his physical closeness the precise expression of his untraversable distance from her, the free air between them a barrier impenetrable as glass. It seemed to her that no one on this earth was more remote from her than this man, sitting less than two feet from her with this, his third fiancée.

But even as she was feeling this, she allowed herself to glance at him for a moment, and at once, in spite of herself, she felt the old ease, the sensation of effortless compatibility.

———

She stopped working at the store soon after that. Neil, who earned a good salary, had been making increasingly scornful remarks about the fact that she chose to work at a mindless job when she didn't need to, and she agreed to quit.

She despised her husband, but the very fact that she had no illusions about this was a source of perverse satisfaction to her; in the irremediable absence of love, it appeared she could make do with someone to hate.

With the new leisure imposed on her, she began cultivating the habits of a pampered mistress. She had their living room furniture reupholstered in raw silk. She bought a pair of Selvaggia shoes for seven hundred dollars. Neil was eager to have a child, and she pretended to want one too, even setting a calendar beside the bed with the optimal nights for conception marked on it. In a morbid ecstasy of self-torture, she allowed him to make love to her on those nights, while privately taking care not to get pregnant.

Meanwhile she subjected her feelings for Kahn to a deliberate effort of destruction, aiming at them an unceasing barrage of self-mockery. They were nothing more than the symptoms of a sickness, she would tell herself, a fixation straight out of some textbook on mental disorders. The relationship between herself and him in that "other" world was a pathetic, one-sided fiction. As for Kahn himself, he was nothing, a cipher onto which she had projected her own romantic fantasies, themselves as shallow and unoriginal as those of some overwrought schoolgirl. What, from any sane point of view, could she possibly want with such a man? Why would she even dream of being involved in the calamitous opera of his life?

Numb, bored, detached even from her own desolation, she drifted on.

One evening she found herself once again at dinner with the friends who had subscribed to Kahn's catalog. She had forgotten about this connection until her neighbor at the table, a young Frenchman, commented on the wine, and she saw again, with a familiar helpless pang, the familiar name on the bottle.

As it turned out, her neighbor and his partner, seated across the table, were in the restaurant business and knew Kahn personally. From the look that passed between them, it was apparent that he was a source of amusing gossip in their world.

Clare glanced at her husband; he was lecturing their host on airline statistics.

"Tell me about Peter Kahn," she said quietly to Jean-Luc, her neighbor.

"Oh! Where to begin!" the young man said with a laugh.

Mark, his American partner, turned to her. "You know him?"

"A little."

Both men grinned at her, their expressions mischievously alert.

"You heard about the wedding?" Jean-Luc asked.

"No."

"Oh my God! Tell her, Mark."

"He was engaged to this model, Diane Wolfe? She was quite famous a few years ago. It was his third marriage, and he told everyone he'd finally found the right woman and to prove it he was going to have the most spectacular romantic wedding, in Venice. They rented a palazzo on the Grand Canal, invited a hundred and fifty guests, hired a jet to fly them over, arranged for the best chef in the Veneto to make the dinner, and had a yacht waiting on the Lido to take the two of them off into the Adriatic for their honeymoon. Well, guess what?"

Clare said nothing. Her heart had begun beating violently.

"He jilted her?" another guest asked.

"At the altar. At the altar. Our friends Sabine and George were there. They told us the whole story. All the guests in the church. . Diane waiting in the back all dressed up in her veils and gown, specially designed, of course, the minutes ticking by, everyone getting steadily more impatient, when this man arrives, a complete stranger, apparently some tourist Peter accosted on the street after his best man refused to do the job, and reads out loud from a piece of paper: 'Ladies and gentlemen, Peter Kahn has asked me to tell you the wedding is canceled. He deeply regrets the pain this will cause . . .' "

Clare listened in a daze.

"What did he do?" she heard herself ask.

"He got out of Venice pretty damn fast, I can tell you!"

"What's he doing now?" The conversation had caught the interest of the rest of the table, and Clare was aware of her husband looking in her direction.

Jean-Luc answered her: "Apparently he's become a bit of a recluse. He sold his business, cut off all his friends. The last we heard he'd moved up to the Finger Lakes, looking to buy some winery of his own."

"Where in the Finger Lakes?" She made a vague effort not to sound too interested.

"I don't know. But we can find out if you like." The young Frenchman's eyes darted mirthfully from Clare to her husband. She could sense, without looking, the way Neil's mouth would be tightening at the corners.

"Can you?"

"Of course."

"I'll give you my e-mail address."

In the taxi home Neil remained silent. The interrogation began as soon as they had closed the door of their apartment behind them. "Why are you so interested in that Kahn guy?"

"No reason."

"Are you planning to visit him or something, up in the Finger Lakes? Is that why you were so eager to get his exact address?"

She shrugged, aware of being infuriating but unable to stop herself.

"I hadn't thought. I was just curious."

"But you don't rule it out? Visiting this man who you apparently hardly know?"

"I don't know, Neil. I haven't thought about it."

Her husband blinked and seemed to reel for a moment. He stood up. She looked away, her eye fixed on a piece of lint on the rug.

"What went on between you and him?"

"What do you mean?"

"You know perfectly well what I mean. He used to come into your store. Right?"

"Yes."

"What for?"

"To buy jewelry."

"Were you having an affair with him?"

"No."

"Look at me when I'm talking, goddammit!"

She felt the sudden crack of his hand on her mouth. She looked up at him.

"All right then," she said.

"What?"

"All right . . . I was."

"What? You were what?"

"Having an affair with him."

Neil's eyes widened. He looked stunned, in spite of himself. She herself was startled by the unexpected potency of her words.

It was as though in saying them she had illuminated some unsuspected truth.

"When? Before we were married or after?"

"Before. And after. He'd come in the store after Ishiro went home." Ishiro was the designer who owned the store. "I'd lock the door, and we'd go up into Ishiro's office."

"And fuck?"

"Yes. Every day. On the chair, on the table——"

A blow struck her on the cheek.

"On the floor——"

Another hit her stomach. She doubled up, covering her face with her hands. Neil was yelling at her, but his words sounded like a foreign language or the roars of an animal. By the time she heard the front door open and slam shut behind him, she was in that glazed world again, as if she had stepped inside a diamond. In it, as vividly as if the scene were happening right there and then, she saw herself in the calm greenness of a summer afternoon, Kahn's gaze opening on her like the sun itself as she approached, silver-blue water glittering in the distance behind him. She uncovered her face. The Finger Lakes, she said to herself. And what remained for her to do seemed clear as day.

LIME PICKLE

Anna's father, not yet divorced, took us out for dinner at the Madras Chop House. In those far-off days it was still a novelty for us to eat in a restaurant, and neither of us had ever eaten at a real Indian restaurant at all. Mr. Hamilton, a dedicated bon viveur, had been shocked to hear this. "Isn't it your birthday coming up?" he had asked Anna. "I shall take you and Matthew to the Madras Chop House."

I picked her up from her school in Hammersmith. I was early, often the case in those days. I had left the same school a year earlier, and aside from a morning job in an art shop, I had very little to do with my time.

I wandered through the school courtyard to the quiet gardens at the back, where I knew Anna would be fencing. There were a dozen or so girls there, practicing their thrusts and parries under the direction of their fencing mistress. Their bendy blunt-tipped foils swished through the crisp spring air and clicked against each other, flashing in the afternoon light. All the girls were dressed in the same fencing outfits, their heads completely covered by their masks, but I recognized Anna immediately. The trim line of her shoulders in the snow-white padded jacket, her boyish hips and slim legs in their tight white breeches like birch saplings in new white bark were unmistakable among the fuller figures of the other girls. As I watched her advance firmly upon her opponent, one hand on her hip, the other in its gauntlet swiveling her foil with fast, graceful, precise movements, I felt the crystalline asperity of her soul sparkle through me like something brilliant and fresh, and I was filled with the still new elation of being in love for the first time.

The fencing ended. Anna took off her mask, and her long dark hair fell down neatly over the white jacket. Seeing me, she smiled and ran over to kiss me on the lips. Her friends waved at me, laughing. In our few months together we had become quite a fixture, faithful, inseparable, the object of good-natured envy and amusement.

After she had showered and changed, we went out onto the Broadway and caught the bus to the West End. Traffic lights and the lit windows of office buildings were beginning to shine against the dusk. When I think now of the peculiar tenderness of our lives at that period, I often find myself remembering these evening bus rides across London: the smell of school soap on Anna's skin, the bristly tartan seats, the conductors lurching down the aisle with their tight black gloves, and out through the windows the city stealthily transforming itself from a thing of bricks and mortar to a little anchored galaxy of electric lights.

I gave Anna her birthday present on the bus. It was a seashell, a nautilus, in flawless condition, heavy and gleaming, as if it had been carved from solid pearl.

"What a beautiful thing, Matthew . . ."

She held it to her ear, then turned it around admiringly, watching its silvery whiteness take on a luster of lilac and emerald from the passing lights. In her quiet way she seemed extremely pleased with it.

"We'll put it on the stone table," she said, "the one overlooking the sea."

In our imaginations we had constructed a house on a Greek island where we were going to live. To the extent that we were in reality planning to spend that summer in Greece, after Anna had finished school, this was not a complete fantasy. Technically we were still virgins then, and "Greece" had come to stand for the time when we would become lovers in the fullest sense. We would find a quiet island in the Aegean. A small hotel by the beach. There, without our having said it in so many words, we would give ourselves finally to each other. For both of us, this image of simple elements—mountains, starlight, sparkling sea—had seemed auspicious.

Darkness had fallen by the time we reached the restaurant. Anna's father arrived just after us, rosy-cheeked from the Garrick, where he conducted most of his business. His portly figure was clad as usual in an elegantly tailored three-piece pinstripe suit, and a silk handkerchief shimmered in his breast pocket.

To our great surprise, he was not alone.

"I'd like you to meet a friend of mine," he said with a faintly embarrassed air, "Lesley McLaughlin."

A woman somewhat younger than himself, in a fur coat with a short mauve alpaca dress and high-heeled leather boots, came forward and offered us each a little cold hand to shake.

"It's a pleasure to meet you," she said with a smile that revealed a row of bright white teeth. Her voice was high and breathy, strangely girlish. Her slightly bouffant hair was partly gathered in a velvet ribbon at the back, falling in a loose, brass-colored sheaf over her padded shoulders.

Anna looked from her to her father. For the past few years, since she had started at her school in London, she and Mr. Hamilton had been living together during the week in a small flat Mr. Hamilton kept in Bayswater, returning at weekends to the house in Suffolk where Mrs. Hamilton lived with her two younger children. It had never occurred to Anna that this arrangement might reflect anything other than convenience. From the slight apprehensive widening in her hazel eyes, it was clear that the woman's presence had begun to rouse her from this dream.

"Lesley lives, ah, not far away," was all Mr. Hamilton offered by way of explanation.

"Yes, I have a little flat in Poland Street," the woman confirmed with an eager smile. "It's literally just around the corner."

"She's a songwriter," Mr. Hamilton said. "And a singer. A marvelous singer."

"Roland, I wish you wouldn't say things like that. You know you don't mean them."

"Oh, but I do. I mean them most sincerely."

We were led to a table deep in the dim crimson-lit interior of the restaurant. Waiters in turbans and embroidered silk jackets moved about with large trays full of lidded salvers. Easing into his favorite role of genial host, Mr. Hamilton assumed an expansive air. He put on a pair of half-moon glasses and inspected the list of aperitifs.

"Splendid," he said. "Let's have a cocktail, shall we? I believe they make an acceptable cocktail here. What do you say? Martinis? Bloody Marys?"

He was a jovial man, at that time quite a successful agent for actors and singers, with an understated shrewdness about him, observable more as a gleam in his eyes than anything he said or did.

Dispatching a waiter with instructions for our drinks, he produced a tissue-wrapped package from his pocket and handed it to his daughter. "A little something for your birthday, darling."

Anna opened the package. Inside was a necklace of linked greenish gold ivy leaves. She looked down at it in silence for a moment.

"It's lovely, isn't it?" Lesley said. "Isn't it the loveliest thing you've ever seen?"

"It's very pretty," Anna replied.

"I told you she'd adore it, didn't I, Roly?"

"You did indeed."

"We were in Asprey's. I said a daughter's only seventeen once. Splurge."

Anna gave her a look of blank incomprehension.

Then she leaned over to kiss her father's cheek. "It's nice, Daddy. Thank you."

"Aren't you going to try it on?" Lesley asked.

"Well, all right."

"Here, let me fasten it for you."

The woman leaned over and fastened the necklace around Anna's neck. Against her girlish cardigan, patterned in rows like an embroidery sampler, it seemed violently incongruous. Even so, it was rather beautiful.

Mr. Hamilton surveyed her, nodding approvingly.

"'Aphrodite, your garlands are made of golden leaves,'" he quoted at her. "Sappho, in case you didn't know."

He spread the menu before him like a general's map, plotting his debauch on our inexperienced palates. The drinks arrived. Mine went straight to my head. I felt alert, pleasantly aware of being in an expensive restaurant. The sound of well-heeled Londoners in full conversational cry, vying with the gulp and throb of a tabla, the moan of a sitar, gave me a sensation of being a part of the rich, swaggering life of the metropolis—not something I often felt in those days. When I drained the last of my cocktail, Mr. Hamilton rewarded me with a connoisseur's nod and smile as if I had accomplished something requiring great technique and sophistication.

"Bravo! Get you another one?"

I was quite drunk by the time the food began arriving. In his usual extravagant fashion, Mr. Hamilton had ordered far more than we could possibly eat. The salvers shoaled at our table till there was no room for any more, and the waiters had to set up an auxiliary camping stool to hold the remainder. Unlidded, the dishes smoked and sizzled, releasing their aromas into the air. Mr. Hamilton spoke knowledgeably about the ingredients of each one as he served us. Words such as fenugreek, cardamom, and asafetida acquired meanings for the first time as I probed the flavors of each dish with my cautiously adventurous tongue. A dish of curried plovers' eggs had been sprinkled with edible gold. "Yes, that's amusing, isn't it, when they do that?" Mr. Hamilton said.

I was acutely susceptible to new sensations in those days; new tastes, new sounds possessed a mystery and resonance entirely unconnected with their objective reality. A dish of lobster tails in a creamy masala sauce arrived. Neither Anna nor I had eaten lobster before. We prized the tails from their dark pink armor as Mr. Hamilton instructed us. As I bit into the succulent flesh, I felt without exaggeration as if I were being led across the threshold into a new universe of delights.

I looked across the table at Anna. She had fallen into a quiet reverie, overwhelmed, it seemed, by the strangeness of the situation: the disturbing presence of her father's friend, the novelty of the food, the fantastical green-gold ivy leaves glittering around her neck. A feeling of tenderness came into me as I gazed at her.

There was something all at once stunned, brave, and delicate in her expression.

At one point Lesley went off to the ladies'. Watching her disappear out of sight, Anna turned to her father, this time with a more pointedly questioning look.

"Ah yes," he said, lowering his eyelids. An embarrassed smile played about his lips. "You're wondering who my friend is. I'm afraid I got rather bludgeoned into bringing her along tonight. I must tell you, though, it was against my better judgment."

He looked up at his daughter.

"Unfortunately, you see, I made the mistake of promising her I'd inform you of our, ah, well, that I'd *tell* you about . . . us. Myself and Lesley, that is. And then last week I'm ashamed to say I told her that I *had* told you, so of course she insisted on my bringing her along to meet you tonight. But of course I *hadn't* told you . . ."

"I see," Anna managed in a subdued voice.

"Now, darling, you're not upset with me, are you?"

"No."

Mr. Hamilton looked at his daughter hesitantly for a moment, before deciding to take her at her word.

"Well, I'm glad that's out in the air, I must say." He patted her on the shoulder and began to grin. "One should never bottle these things up, you know. Bad for the digestion." He smoothed his napkin and adjusted the flamelike triangle of his silk handerchief. "Now, if you don't mind, I'd rather we weren't discussing this when Lesley returns. She can be extremely touchy, and it mightn't go down too well if she cottons on that I hadn't mentioned her to you till now."

In the silence that followed, a sudden mischievous expression appeared on his face.

"Here," he said, "I don't think you've tried this yet, have you?"

He scooped us each a spoonful of something from a small dish at the center of the table.

"Eat the whole thing"—he encouraged—"go on, you'll enjoy it."

As soon as we put the spoons in our mouths a violent sourness and fieriness burst on our tongues. It was as if he had given us each a red-hot coal to eat, or a spoonful of hydrochloric acid.

"Lime pickle," he said, and burst into laughter.

———

At the end of the meal he wanted us to come back to Lesley's flat and listen to her sing. We made our way through Soho, Mr. Hamilton leading us at a stately pace, surveying everything we passed—the bead-curtained strip clubs with miniskirted hostesses beckoning us in, the porn-shingled shopwindows—with leisurely, unabashed interest. Lesley clopped along next to him, keeping up an incessant flow of soft chatter, which he largely ignored.

Anna was beside me, clinging to my arm. Her school satchel hung from her other shoulder, in it the nautilus we were going to put on the stone table in our island house. The ivy leaves tinkled strangely at her neck as she walked.

We went into a newish brick building and climbed a flight of stairs to a door that Lesley opened. Her flat was done up in flowery pastel materials with a lot of flounces and ruched trimmings. There were lace-edged cushions everywhere and a row of costumed dolls on a shelf. In one corner was an electric piano.

Anna and I sat on a sofa while Mr. Hamilton poured us each a drink. Lesley turned the lights low and, after the obligatory show of bashfulness, struck up a tune on the electric piano and began to sing.

Her voice wasn't bad—husky and surprisingly low—but to our fastidious, intolerant ears, the songs themselves (Broadway ballads mostly, as far as I can remember) were unbearable. While she sang them, which she did in an American accent, she went through a routine of stiff, exaggerated expressions. She batted her eyelids, tossed her head, puckered her mouth to look "wry," doggedly illustrating whatever the lyrics suggested, as if she had a foreign or perhaps deaf audience in mind. Mr. Hamilton clapped at the end of each number, defiantly unfazed. At one point she sang a song with a chorus that went "Because he teases me he pleases me," gazing at him lovingly. Anna looked at her father as if in expectation of—what? A complicit wink? An acknowledgment that all this was at the very least an aberration? But he studiously avoided her eye. Even in my inebriated state I felt the painfulness of the situation. Anna clung to me tightly as if to protect herself. I felt her perplexity, her slight fear and horror as she leaned against me. It was as if she were watching the seventeen years of her family life at the Suffolk millhouse, with all its civilized entertainments and innocent rituals, dissolve in some corrosive solution before her eyes.

"You're going to be a star, my dear. I feel it absolutely," Mr. Hamilton said as Lesley finished.

"Oh, Roland, it's so tiresome when you flatter me. He's forever trying to flatter me. But I never believe him. I'm afraid I've got his number."

Mr. Hamilton stood up. "I'll tell you what. Why don't we leave these two here and us jump into a taxi? Anna looks ready for bed, and Matthew, I'm sure, doesn't want to slog all the way up to Wood Green at this time of night, do you, dear boy?"

"Well—"

Lesley broke in. "Of course! What a good idea. There's everything you need right here. I'll get you some towels, but I put on clean sheets just this morning."

Mr. Hamilton turned a little uncertainly to his daughter. "How does that suit you, darling one?"

Anna looked at him helplessly. She seemed to have taken in about all she could absorb in one night.

"All right."

Fluffy pink towels were produced. We were shown the floral bedroom, the warm, windowless bathroom, where the gleaming chrome snake of a handheld shower had coiled itself over the taps of a vast oval bath.

Then they were gone.

That was twenty years ago. Last month I read Mr. Hamilton's obituary in *The Times*. By then his wife had divorced him, and between his own expensive tastes and those of Lesley and her successors, he had bankrupted himself. For a while he lived at the Bayswater flat, then moved into a series of increasingly seedy hotels.

A few years ago I visited Anna at her house in Muswell Hill. She herself was divorced then, with two teenage children, one of them in trouble with drugs. Dirty washing up was piled in the sink, and a great tidal stain of damp had spread across the ceiling. Exhausted, though stout and surprisingly robust-looking, Anna told me how her father had taken to "dropping in" on her for days, and then weeks, at a time. He had become shabby and cantankerous and was often drunk, and although she felt sorry for him, she found his presence in the house increasingly hard to bear. Finally she had had to ask him to leave.

As I read his obituary, I found myself thinking once again of our night out at the Madras Chop House. I remembered the casually debonair way in which he had turned up with his girlfriend, the gilded ivy necklace he'd given Anna and how it tinkled disconcertingly as we walked through Soho. I thought of Lesley's songs and Mr. Hamilton's furtive charade of pleasure as he listened to them, and of course I remembered their abrupt departure, leaving Anna and me alone for the night. It was the first time we had been in a position to spend the night together, but the circumstances had left us more depressed than elated. Everything estranged us: the sugared decor of Lesley's flat; the evening's vast, if barely acknowledged, revelations; the unexpected freedom the night had thrust upon us. A heart-shaped satin cushion lay on the bed. The sheets were scented. We undressed and climbed in, holding each other tightly in an attempt to retrieve our companionable intimacy. I remembered the thin, curiously irrelevant feeling of desire that came into me. Anna looked at me with her frail, still rather stunned expression. "No," she said, "no, not now. In the summer . . ." But a short while later we were no longer virgins.

And I remembered too the spoonful of lime pickle Mr. Hamilton tricked us into eating, his laughter as it burned on our astounded tongues—harsh, caustic, not altogether benign—his shoulders shaking, his eyes watering with pleasure almost as much as ours had with pain. At the time the joke had seemed to me merely stupid and cruel, but as I remember it now, I find myself curiously amused by it. An involuntary smile twists itself into my face. A gravelly chuckle begins to rise in my throat. Tears come into my eyes . . .

Before I left Anna's house in Muswell Hill, she took me up into her bedroom, saying she wanted to show me something. There on the mantelpiece, gleaming palely in the gray London light, was the nautilus I had given her for her seventeenth birthday. She and I had kept in touch over the years, though we had little in common other than an increasingly small proportion of our pasts. Perhaps I misconstrued her gesture in bringing me upstairs, but I felt awkward standing there, and my reaction on seeing the shell—still there in her life, still intact—was in all truth one of suffocating oppression. As delicately as I could, I made my excuses and left.

I haven't seen her since.

IT'S BEGINNING TO HURT

"Good lunch, Mr. Bryar?"

"Excellent lunch."

"Sorleys?"

"No, some . . . Chinese place."

"Your wife rang."

He dialed home; his wife answered:

"Where on earth have you been?"

"Sorry, darling. Complicated lunch . . ."

Strange, to be lying to her once again. And about a funeral!

"Tom's coming down. Stop at Dalgliesh's—would you?—and pick up a salmon. A wild one? Better go right now, actually, in case they run out."

It was July, a baking summer. He walked slowly, thinking of the ceremony he had just attended. Among the half dozen mourners, he had known only the solicitor who had introduced him to Marie ten years ago and had told him of her death last week. The news had stunned him; he hadn't known she was ill, but then he hadn't seen her for seven years. Throughout the service he had found himself weeping uncontrollably.

The man at Dalgliesh's hoisted a fish the length of his arm from under a covering of seaweed and ice.

"How's that?"

"Okay. Would you—"

"Gut her and clean her, sir?"

"Please."

The man slit the creature's belly with a short knife, spilling the dewy beige guts into a bucket. He rinsed the flecked mesh of scales and the red flesh inside, then wrapped the fish in paper and put it in a plastic bag.

It was six inches too long for the office fridge.

"Bugger."

He went down to the stockroom. There were glue traps lying about with dead mice and beetles on them, but it was cooler there than upstairs. Uneasily, he placed the fish in the drawer of an old metal filing cabinet.

For the rest of the afternoon he worked on new rental listings. His eyes were burning when he stopped. It was late, and he had to hurry to the tube station. Sweating and panting, he emerged at Charing Cross just in time to get the six-forty.

On the train, crowded with weekenders, he found himself thinking of Marie. They couldn't afford hotels, so they used to pretend she was a client, interested in one of the properties listed with his firm. Every home they entered was a different world. Making love in the "sumptuously appointed Victorian maisonette" or the "cozy garden flat" was an adventure into a series of possible lives, each with its own reckless joys: one afternoon they were rich socialites; the next a pair of bohemian students . . . For three years he had felt the happiest man alive, and the luckiest. Marie never asked him to leave his family, and he had regarded this too as part of his luck. And then, abruptly, she had ended it. "I'm in love with you," she'd told him matter-of-factly, "and it's beginning to hurt."

His wife was waiting for him outside the station.

"Where's the salmon?" she asked.

A sudden horror spread through him.

"I—I left it behind."

She turned abruptly away, then stared back at him a moment.

"You're a fool," she said. "You're a complete bloody fool."

CATERPILLARS

At first they thought the white things in the trees were plastic bags. You saw that back in Brooklyn all the time, scraps of sheeny litter caught in the branches of sidewalk ginkgoes and sycamores. But out here in the middle of the French countryside it was a shock.

"Human beings," Craig said calmly, "are disgusting."

But as they came closer, they saw that what they were looking at were in fact cocoons, with shadows of caterpillars moving inside them.

The trees were pines, and the caterpillars had anchored their cocoons to the bendy twigs of different branches, using them for tension like the guy ropes of marquees. Clusters of needles had been trapped and flattened under the skeins of milky webbing.

Craig peered in at them. "I guess it's some kind of tent caterpillar."

Caitlin smiled cautiously. "Oh well. At least it's not people . . ."

He shrugged; it wasn't his style to recant.

Luke, his son, poked at one of the cocoons with a stick. The branches moved, but the dense, opaque fibers stayed intact. He poked again, harder.

"Don't do that," Craig told him.

They walked on, passing through vineyards and a long orchard of almond trees. On the far side of this they came to another stand of pines with the cocoons in them. There were more of them this time, and the trees looked more blighted than the others, the branches around the webby fabric drooping downward, with clusters of dead brown needles dangling from their twigs. The three hurried on past.

At lunchtime they picnicked under a stone watchtower on a hill. The trees up there were oaks and birches, and there were no cocoons in them. But when they moved on, turning onto the trail that led back to the hotel, they passed again through pinewoods, and there were white cocoons lodged in the green branches wherever they looked. Around each one, large volumes of needles had desiccated and turned brown. Inside, among the moving shapes of caterpillars, were strangled clusters of brown needles showing milkily through. Dead branches hung crookedly from the trunks. On some of the trees there were ten or twelve cocoons in different places.

Caitlin turned to Luke. "They look sort of like invalids, don't they, the trees? Covered in bandages?"

The boy gave her the unnerving sidelong look that had so far greeted most of her attempts to befriend him.

Back at the hotel the owner told them the cocoons were made by processionary caterpillars, "*chenilles processionnaires.*" They were called that, he explained, because they traveled in long lines joined head to toe. Most years the winter killed enough of them that they weren't a problem, but the past few winters had been warm, so now there was an infestation. He smiled as he said this, as if it were something to be proud of.

Craig asked if they were everywhere in this area. The man nodded enthusiastically. "*Ici, oui, partout.*"

Wagging a finger, he added: "*Faut pas les toucher...*" You shouldn't touch them, or you could get a painful rash.

They had been planning to do another walk from the village
the next day, to a cave with an underground lake. But after this
conversation Craig said it would be too depressing to spend another day surrounded by half-dead trees and that they should leave
early in the morning instead.

"Let's head on up to the mountains."

"What about the cave?" Luke asked.

"There'll be other things to see."

So the next morning they drove to the mountains. Their ears
popped as they climbed. The air grew cooler. Vineyards gave way
to stony lavender fields and sheep pastures bounded by low stone
walls. Above these a vast pine forest began.

The three fell silent, staring out through the windows. The
trees looked healthy enough, tall and straight, their branches
spreading a pelt of deep, dark green over the bony ridges and
slopes of the mountains. On the steepest slopes the trees grew
more sparsely, and you could see the gray mountainside rubble between them, but even in these places they seemed to be flourish-
ing, their massive, upward-curving branches bearing thick swaths
of unblemished black-green needles.

Only as the forest became interspersed with pasture again did
Caitlin see a cocoon, just the one, glistening like a tuft of cotton
candy high in the branches of a tree above the road. She didn't say
anything; the others seemed not to have noticed.

The road turned to gravel, following a shallow river until it arrived at the stone buildings of the farm where they were staying.
After they had checked in and eaten lunch, Craig spread out the
hiking map. There was a pair of *bergeries* in the area that he
wanted to see; old drystone sheepcotes that had been designated
historic sites. According to the guidebook, you could get to them
only on foot, which was a part of their attraction as far as Craig
was concerned. They were set below a high ridge, and the woman

who ran the farm restaurant pointed out a ringwalk they could do that would bring them past each *bergerie* before circling back to the farm in time for dinner.

The first part of the trail led over a saddle of grassland with sheep grazing on it. There were no pylons or cell phone towers to upset Craig, and for this Caitlin was grateful. Not that she liked these things any more than he did, but his diatribes had an unsettling effect on her. Since being with Craig, she had found that it was necessary to guard, rather carefully, what remained of her affection for her own species.

Over the saddle the trail fell through a valley to a stream where it entered a dark wood of deciduous trees. The stream was deep in places, with pools of green water under ledges of moss-covered rock. Along its banks were patches of buttery yellow that turned out to be primroses. There were also purple flowers that Craig said were hepatica.

"It's nice here," Caitlin ventured.

"Not bad," Craig agreed.

As they came out of the wood and began climbing again, they saw something on the path ahead of them that appeared to be a long dark snake, moving very slowly forward over the red dust.

Luke ran toward it.

"It's the caterpillars!"

They walked up and stood over the creatures. They were an inch and a half long, gray, with an orange stripe along the top, and covered with pale spikes of fur. Each shiny black head was attached to the tail of the caterpillar in front. Their progress along the path was slow, but the quilted, rubbery pouches of their bodies moved in vigorous undulations.

Craig squatted down. After inspecting them closely for some time, he called to his son. "Come here, Luke."

The boy squatted beside him.

"We don't kill animals, do we?"

"No. Mom does. She kills mice."

"Okay, but I don't and you don't and Caitlin doesn't. But these animals, I'm thinking—they aren't part of nature, exactly. They're here because the winters haven't been cold enough to kill them, and you know why that is, right?"

The boy thought for a moment.

"Oh," he said in a dull voice, "global warming."

"Right. Which makes them partly a human phenomenon. Now, look at those pine trees." Craig pointed to the wooded ridge ahead of them. "These guys can probably smell them from here. I imagine it's a good smell to them. They're going to go up there and start making their cocoons, which means pretty soon that whole forest is going to be infested like the one we saw yesterday."

The boy blinked, then gave a grin.

"Are we going to kill them, Dad?"

"Yes, we are. But I want to make sure you understand why. Do you?"

"Yes, yes. How are we going to do it?"

"Like this."

Craig stood up and stamped on the first caterpillar in the column, bursting it under the thick sole of his hiking boot. The line started breaking apart immediately, each individual uncoupling itself and striking out in its puff of fur with an appearance of panicky disorientation. The boy jumped on a group of them, crushing them to a dark pulp in the dust. Then he and Craig proceeded to obliterate the entire column.

"That takes care of that," Craig said.

But a little farther along the trail they came upon another procession, crawling slowly up toward the ridge. This time father and son set about destroying them without any discussion, Luke yelling gleefully as he jumped about, Craig preserving a neutral

air, as if he regarded himself as the instrument of some purely impersonal force of necessity.

They didn't see any more caterpillars after that. The path
climbed through an area of the sweet-smelling scrub of juniper
and wild rosemary they had learned to call *garigue*. Luke and
Craig were chatting, at ease with each other for the first time in
days. Caitlin walked behind them, conscious of the need to give
them their space.

As their trail turned for the final, steepest part of the ascent,
they saw something shiny rising toward them over the brow of the
ridge, a couple of hundred yards ahead. It was a car, a silver
SUV—the small kind they had here in France—and it was driving down the footpath. A moment later another one, identical, appeared behind it, then another, and then another. Very slowly the
four vehicles came down the near vertical-looking top section of
the trail, before turning onto the horizontal path that branched off
along the ridge toward the *bergeries*. There, in tight convoy, dust
puffing up from their tires, they rolled slowly onward, disappearing into the trees.

"What the fuck was that?" Craig said.

He unfolded his map.

"They're on a footpath," he said. "There's no road there, and
there's no road on the other side where they came from either." He
folded the map back up, quickening his pace toward the ridge as if
he thought he might be able to catch up with the cars. They were
out of sight, of course, by the time the three of them reached the
intersection. But the smell of their exhaust hung in the air, and
you could still hear the sound of their engines over the tinkle of
sheep bells down in the valley.

"They're driving on a goddamn footpath!" Craig said.

They took the same turning as the cars had taken. Once they
entered the woods they saw that there were in fact cocoons all over

the pine trees. Caitlin glanced at Craig, but he didn't seem interested in pursuing the implications of this. His jaw was set tight,
his gray eyes glaring ahead along the trail. His bearing, as always,
was calm, but she could tell he was furious. He would have liked to
crush the cars, she sensed, just as he had crushed the caterpillars.
Suddenly he stepped off the path into the woods. He stooped down
for something, then came out backward, dragging the bleached
trunk of a fallen tree.

"Luke, give me a hand!"

The boy helped his father drag the tree across the footpath.

"What are we doing?"

"We're giving those people something to think about when
they come back from their expedition. A little roadblock."

"Oh. Cool."

"In fact maybe a series of roadblocks," Craig said, scanning
the woods again. "Make sure they get the point. It'll be like those
stations of the cross they had outside that first village. Some little
opportunities for reflection. There's another tree . . ."

He and Luke dragged out several other trees as they walked
along, setting them across the path every fifty yards or so. Caitlin
looked on, unsure this was a good idea, but not wanting to get into an
argument. With Craig you had to be utterly convinced of your position if you wanted to disagree with him, and she suspected her mis-
givings might be nothing more than cowardice. Besides, she didn't
want to interfere when he and Luke were getting along like this.

At one point they found some large rocks.

"We'll use these too," Craig said.

He and Luke braced themselves against the rocks, maneuver-
ing them into the middle of the path.

A little farther along they saw a tractor tire lying by a gate at
the entrance to a field. They heaved it up on its edge. It was enormous, almost as wide in diameter as Luke was tall. Together they

rolled it into the path, where they tipped it over, water splatting from a gash in its side as it fell.

"Okay," Craig said. "That should do the trick."

They walked on along the flat, stony path. After a while Luke began lagging behind.

"Wait for me!" he shouted.

"Keep up," Craig called back. "We have a ways to go."

It was another half hour before they arrived at the first *bergerie*. The four cars were parked in a line at the top of the steeply sloping meadow, in the middle of which stood the small domed and arched sheepcote and shepherd's hut. A group of people stood outside, gathered around a large woman in an outfit of mauve tweed.

"I'll wait here for Luke, shall I?" Caitlin said at the entrance to the meadow. The boy had fallen back again. Craig shrugged, then walked on down.

She watched him approach the buildings. Several faces from the group turned toward him with smiles of greeting, and she watched his tall, straight figure stride past them into one of the buildings without so much as a glance in their direction. She couldn't see his face, but she knew the severe expression it would be wearing. A familiar half-fearful, half-admiring feeling came into her as she pictured it. She found it so difficult herself to judge other people's behavior, even when she could see it was wrong. But Craig regarded it as an obligation. He had told her once that if he'd been born in a time when it was possible to believe in a god, he would have felt compelled to become a preacher. He had gone into furniture making instead, but even this he had turned into his own kind of crusade, with his recycled materials, his all-natural stains and varnishes, his rejection of all elements of ornamentation and superfluous comfort from his designs. "It's what Jesus would have done if he'd stuck to carpentry," he liked to joke. Or not joke exactly, just say with a glint in his eye that you felt you were permitted to take as humorous. She'd never been with a man quite like him before. She didn't love him exactly, not in the usual way of wanting to be always kissing and fooling around together. She didn't even like him, she sometimes thought, observing his cold manner with people he disapproved of, which was most of the human race. But he had engulfed her somehow, taken up residence in her imagination like some large, dense, intractable problem that had been given to her to solve.

By the time Luke caught up, the group had begun walking back up toward their cars. The woman in the mauve outfit was talking to them in English, with a French accent:

"What you will see at the next *bergerie* will be a completely different technique of construction. Instead of the vaulted ceilings we have here, you will see that it will be built in the tunnel style . . ."

The people were mostly middle-aged, some of the men wearing ties and sport coats under green waterproof jackets, the women in wool and tweed outfits like their guide, though in more subdued colors. They looked like professors, Caitlin thought. They smiled at her, and she smiled uncomfortably back, wishing that she weren't having to encounter them like this, in person.

The guide gave her a polite nod as she passed. Her eye lingered a moment on Luke. Caitlin looked back and saw that the boy had lifted his T-shirt over his large belly, which he was scratching vigorously. It was a bit embarrassing, but she didn't feel it was her place to tell him to stop. Up beyond him the people were climbing back into their cars.

Craig emerged from the dark interior of the sheep shelter. He stood in the entrance, watching the cars as they set off in a line along the footpath, heading for the second *bergerie*.

"I was thinking," he said, "if they were in wheelchairs or something, that might be an excuse, but really I don't even believe that. It's not like if I was old or disabled, I'd feel entitled to be driven places off the road that I couldn't walk to. Anyway, those people are perfectly capable of walking. They're just lazy and selfish."

They wandered through the buildings. Craig explained how the arches and domed roofs were built without any tools or cement, just with the careful piling and balancing of all the flattest stones the shepherds could find in the area. There was a rare note of approval in his voice, and Caitlin brightened, as she always did at such moments. He loved this kind of patient, anonymous craftsmanship, and his enthusiasm when he spoke about it made her want to cheer him on even though she didn't find it that exciting herself.

After they had finished looking, they went back to the path and started walking to the second *bergerie*. The boy was scratching himself again.

"What are you doing?" Craig asked.

"It itches."

"Leave it alone. What is it, a mosquito bite?"

He peered at his son's stomach. "I don't see anything. Except too much of this." He grabbed the roll of fat on Luke's belly. "Come on, let's burn some off."

He set off at a brisk march. The boy soon started lagging behind again.

"Wait!"

Craig turned. "Keep up, kiddo. And stop the scratching."

The boy was panting when he caught up. His face was mottled pink.

"I can't walk this fast," he said. He was scratching his forearms now, clawing them with his plump, nail-bitten fingers.

"What is going on?" Craig said.

"I don't know."

"Well, stop scratching. And try to keep up." He tousled the boy's hair. "You want a nature quiz?"

"No."

They walked in silence along the path. The sun had dropped below the other side of the ridge, and they were in shadow now. Here and there pale cocoons hung in the pines above them, stretched and bulging in a way that made Caitlin think of something hawked up from a lung. She tried not to look. Before long the boy had fallen behind again.

"Wait for me!" he wailed.

This time when he caught up, his face was an angry red and there were yellowish welts standing out on his arms.

"My God," Caitlin said, "are you okay?"

He ignored her, as usual. Craig examined his arms.

"It looks like hives. He gets allergies sometimes. You didn't touch one of those caterpillars, did you? With your skin?"

"No."

"Well, listen, we're not halfway yet. We have another couple hours' walking. Think you can make it okay?"

"I don't feel good."

"I know. We'll get you some antihistamine when we get back. But you're okay to go on, right?"

"I'm tired."

"I could take him back the way we came," Caitlin heard herself say, "I mean, if you want to go on . . ."

"No!" the boy said, clinging to his father.

Craig opened the map. He didn't say anything for a while.

"How much shorter would it be?" Caitlin asked.

"To go back?"

"Mm."

He looked at her; a faint sardonic light in his eye, as if in acknowledgment of some small but unexpected challenge.

"A bit. Yeah, I guess it would be quite a bit shorter."

He looked again at Luke. The boy seemed dazed. The soft flesh around his eyes had begun to swell up, and the eyes themselves were bloodshot.

"All right," Craig said, folding the map away. "We'll go back. We'll go back the way we came."

And so they turned around and started walking back along the trail the way they had come. This time they moved at Luke's pace; it took them a good twenty minutes to reach the *bergerie* again, twice as long as it had coming.

"Can we have a rest?" the boy said as they passed above the buildings. He was panting heavily.

"No. We should keep going now."

"But I'm tired. My eyes hurt."

"Come on."

The boy stood still on the path. "I can't!" His lip trembled. "I'm not walking anymore!"

Craig stared down at him. "Okay," he said. "Get on my shoulders."

He stooped down, and the boy climbed on his shoulders. Slowly, with a slight backward lurch, Craig stood up, his thin frame looking perilously top-heavy under its burden.

"Christ," he muttered.

They walked on along the path, their progress even slower than before. Luke huddled over his father, resting a swollen cheek on his head. The air was cool, but after a while beads of sweat began to slide down over Craig's face. A vein stood out on his forehead. He looked at Caitlin. "I'm not going to be able to carry him all the way."

She nodded, saying nothing. There was nothing she could think of to say.

A few minutes after this she heard the cars, returning along

the trail behind them. She had been listening for them, but even
so, a feeling of dread came into her. It seemed to sink through her,
twisting slowly as it fell, like some heavy object drifting down
through oil. As they drew near, Luke raised his head and turned
back groggily to look. His eyes were thin red slits in the cushions
of flesh around them. Craig moved to the side of the path but
went on walking steadily forward, acknowledging nothing.

It occurred to Caitlin that he wasn't going to be able to ask the
people for a ride. She could feel, as if she were him for a moment,
the impossibility of it. He couldn't carry the boy all the way, but he
would break his back trying rather than ask these people for help.
At the same time he must have been able to see that that would
solve nothing. Dimly it seemed to her that somewhere in the stubborn grid of his thoughts there must be a calculation that she
would do the asking, that if she did, it would be possible to accept.
A part of her rebelled at being counted on like this. For a moment
she was tempted not to play along, just to see what he would do.
But even as she tried to assume the necessary attitude of indifference, she knew that his calculation was correct: that she didn't
have the heart for it. She turned to face the cars, smiling helplessly
and putting out her hand to stop them. As it happened, they were
stopping anyway, and the driver's window of the front car was sliding down.

"*Il est malade, le petit?*" came the voice of the guide.

"Excuse me?"

"Your child is sick?"

"Yes, yes, he's sick!" Caitlin said, then shouted: "Can you help
us? Craig! Stop!"

Craig swung slowly around, his face streaming sweat now.

The guide got out of the car, looking up at Luke.

"What happened to him?"

Caitlin answered: "We don't know. We think some kind of allergy . . ."

"I thought this when I saw him before. Did he go near to some of the caterpillars who make these nests?" She pointed up into the trees.

"He was near them, but he didn't touch them."

"You don't need to touch. Even if you just go near to them and breathe the air, it can be dangerous. Especially for the eyes." She came close to where Craig stood with the boy on his shoulders. "Ah! But you must bring him to the hospital immediately! Come with us. We'll drive you."

Craig said nothing, but he lifted Luke from his shoulders. The guide took charge, installing the three of them in the backseat. A gray-haired couple moved over to make room for them. In the passenger seat in front was a man with a shrewd, pointed face. He and the couple made sympathetic noises to Luke as the woman led the convoy off again. The boy buried his head in his father's shoulder.

"Where are you staying?" the guide asked. She was driving fast, much faster than she had before.

Caitlin named the farm.

"Ah. This side of the mountain. The hospital is on the other side. You'll have to take a taxi after you—"

She slammed on the brakes: *"Mais c'est quoi—?"*

They had come to the tractor tire.

"I'll move it," Craig said, opening his door. Passengers got out of the cars behind. Caitlin thought she should stay in the car with Luke, even though the boy wriggled free when she tried to hold him. She watched the people help Craig move the enormous tire, laughter and puzzlement on their faces as they returned to their cars. She heard someone say a farmer must have dropped it. Craig climbed back into his seat and stared fixedly out through the window. Caitlin's heart was beating fast, almost fluttering in her chest, as the car started up and they sped off once more.

"Are you all professors?" she asked. "Is that why you're—"

"Heavens, no!" The man in front chuckled.

The woman of the couple spoke: "We're members of a rural preservation group from Suffolk. We go on a jaunt somewhere abroad every year."

Again the guide slammed on the brakes.

"*Mais . . . !*"

They had come to the rocks.

Craig was out of the car almost before it had stopped. Others got out to help him once again. This time there was less laughter. The man in the front seat looked at Caitlin in the mirror. She turned away, blushing. He said something very fast in French to the guide as they set off again. The woman looked disbelieving, but at the first of the fallen trees she stopped more gradually, as if half expecting it. Craig jumped out, and this time only a couple of people from the cars behind came to help him. At the next tree nobody came. The four cars stood with their engines idling while he dragged the heavy, skeletal trunk back into the woods. Then they rolled slowly forward to the next, where he got out again. He was armoring himself, it appeared, in a kind of stoical detachment. But for Caitlin the situation was unfolding with excruciating vividness. She watched him get out and move the remaining obstacles, one after another. Alone on the path he seemed to her a strange, parched, remote, beleaguered figure. His face was expressionless, but the straining muscles at his neck and the sweat on his face as he dragged the dead trunks across the dust and stones gave him an agonized look. She felt a desire to comfort him, even though she knew he would have repudiated any hint of pity. Climbing back into his seat after the final tree, he took out a handkerchief and mopped his face. The guide looked at him in the mirror.

"That's the last one?" she asked.

He stared back at her a moment.

Then he nodded, and she drove on.

Nobody spoke after that. Caitlin felt the silence bearing down on her. What made it worse was that there was nowhere to look that gave any relief. Craig, Luke, the guide, the other passengers, the trees outside hung with their cocoons: everything seemed to add its own oppressive weight to the moment.

At the intersection they turned right and crossed over to the far side of the ridge. The valley below them was much larger than the one they had crossed on the way from the farm, and it was built up. Houses began halfway down the slope opposite, scattered thinly at first, but growing more dense toward the bottom, their lights hanging pale against the gray-green hillside. Caitlin glanced at Craig, then flinched away. She told herself that the hospital was down there, that these people helping them had also come from down there somewhere. But it was impossible not to think of the cocoons. She closed her eyes, but even then she could see them: pale shapes in the darkness behind her own eyelids, with the shadows of the caterpillars crawling around inside them.